The Story of My Scars

by Victoria Perkins

For Chrissy and Angela
Thank you for sharing your
creativity with me and allowing
me to share it with others.
I'm blessed to have both of
you in my life.

Introduction to the collection

I don't write short stories much anymore, but I wanted to put together the short stories I'd written as companions or sequels to some of my novels, so I gathered those, as well as some old and new short work to put together for this collection. Unlike my previous collection, this one contains a variety of different works, not only short stories. Much more diverse than my prior collection, I hope there's something here for everyone.

Introduction to "The Story of My Scars"

I'd originally intended this to be a full novel, but as I began the story and figured out where it would end, I realized that it needed to be a short story instead. I always have a hard time with titles, but this was one where I knew what I wanted the title to be from moment one, so when I decided to put the short stories into a collection, it made sense to use the same title for the whole collection.

"The Story of My Scars"

RIKI

I have a two-inch scar along my hairline where, when I was three, I cut my head on some toilet paper. Well, the ceramic holder anyway. On my right shin, I have a mass of scar tissue approximately the size of a quarter. An active child, I'd fallen out of my cousin's hickory tree and the resulting broken bone had pushed through the skin. My left foot has scars on both its bottom and top from when I was twelve. My cat, Sookie, knocked over our Christmas tree. A shard of what had once been a pair of frolicking reindeer went in the sole of my foot and came out the top. From the base of my neck to the small of my back is covered with thin white lines, an intricate pattern of whirls and shapes.

I'm seventeen and those scars first appeared yesterday morning, my birthday. I don't know what happened.

****

I scowled into the mirror, the impression staring back at me more tabby kitten than ferocious lion. I hadn't pulled back my hair yet and it spilled over my shoulders, a cascade of curls the shade of molten lava. Thanks to a sunny summer, my skin was a mass of freckles, but even they couldn't hide the chaos my back had become yesterday morning.

I'd panicked then, running to my mother with tears streaming down my cheeks. She'd hadn't said a word, but I hadn't known if she'd been intentionally ignoring me or if it had just been the large amounts of Jack Daniels she'd just consumed. Her drinking had gone from social to out-of-control after Cici had died.

Died might not have been the best word for what happened. Cici had been murdered, and my mother hadn't forgiven me for letting it happen. Not that I blamed her. I hadn't forgiven myself either.

I tried to push the memory to the back of my mind and focus on the task at hand: finding a shirt cool enough to wear while still covering the mysterious marks on my skin. After I'd made my choice and finished dressing, I double-checked my outfit. The cobalt-blue tank top was the same shade as my eyes, but I was more concerned with the edges of marred skin I could still see. It was too hot for my hair to be down. The heavy braid covered the back of my neck, but my shoulders were still exposed.

Oh, well. I was hunting for a killer, not going to prom. I wasn't trying to impress anyone. I had work to do. To start, I was going to the library.

I knew what had happened to Cici, at least in some part of my brain. I'd been there six nights ago, but I only remembered the screams from the darkness, the shadow emerging from the woods. My sister's face, pale in the moonlight, staring at me for a split second before the shadow had pulled her out of the tent.

Then, nothing until the wail of sirens splitting the forest air. The police who'd taken the statements of everyone who'd been camping within a ten-mile radius, including the two of us who'd been at the center of the bloodbath. The handsome young man with the ice gray eyes who had been the only other survivor.

A group of hikers had found Cici three days later.

JENSON

My first fist-fight had resulted in a broken nose, three black eyes, several split lips and a total of forty-seven stitches. Twelve of those were mine. Apparently, Robbie Shinar's shattered front teeth'd had some bite. My knuckles and bloody lip had been my only injuries that day, but they hadn't been the last. With a name like mine, the rash of scars on my knuckles weren't a surprise. I also had a line through one eyebrow where an overenthusiastic spectator had landed a lucky blow with a jar of baby food – don't ask. The torn up skin on my knees had been the result of too many skateboarding accidents as a daredevil preteen.

It was the strange criss-crossing scars that covered my entire torso that really freaked me out.

****

I'd read the same article about five times, but I couldn't seem to make myself stop. I brushed a chunk of hair out of my eyes, irritated by its length. I knew I could ask Irina to cut it, but since Alexei had disappeared six days ago, I hadn't been able to face my stepmother. I didn't know if she blamed me, but I blamed myself enough for everyone.

I felt a presence before I heard the sharp intake of breath, so I turned around in time to see the still-wide eyes of a striking young woman. Recognition hit me a second later and all air rushed from my lungs. I'd seen her just once before. July twenty-ninth, right after my half-brother had vanished.

"You – you're..."

She recognized me too. I stood and took a step towards her. "Jenson Coppenhagen."

Technically, that was right. I wasn't about to give her my real name. When your biological mother had been a philosophy major, being named Aristotle Socrates wasn't exactly a shock. It didn't really make it more appealing, however. My name was pretty much all I had of her, but there was a connection with my nickname too. My Russian-born nanny – before she'd become my stepmother – hadn't been able to pronounce my name, so she'd referred to me as Jen's son until it'd come together as Jenson...and stuck.

Her hand was cool, but steady, as it clasped mine. "Riki Shale."

I was pretty sure that was her actual name, and it suited

her.

I motioned to the empty chair behind me. I knew her reason for being here was linked to mine because I'd placed her name as well. Her sibling, however, wasn't missing anymore. I wasn't sure which was worse, the not knowing, or what had happened to her little sister. The funeral was tomorrow.

Her eyes fell to the paper as she slid into the rickety chair. The periodical section of the Fort Prince local library wasn't exactly the most comfortable room, especially the secluded section where I'd sequestered myself.

I settled back into my seat, studying my fellow survivor with genuine curiosity. I hadn't paid much attention to her before and, I assumed, she'd been likewise preoccupied at the time. I was surprised to realize how striking she was. Even under the florescent lights, her hair burned, shimmered. My gaze traveled down her body and I felt a jolt of electricity as I reached her shoulders. She shifted self-consciously and I forced myself to look away. It had to be a coincidence.

"Any word on your brother?" Her voice was low, gentle.

I shook my head, unsure if I was more surprised by her concern or the stinging in my eyes that accompanied my reaction. "I think they've pretty much given up even though it's been less than a week. They all think he's dead because..."

Idiot.

King of idiots.

"Because of Cici." Her half-smile broke my heart more than crying would have.

I opened my mouth to apologize. To offer every platitude I could imagine to make up for my total thoughtlessness. Perhaps literally putting my foot in my mouth could rectify the situation.

She shook her head before I could speak. "You're trying to find him, aren't you? Your brother, I mean." At my nod, she continued, "Let me help."

I could read the reasons in the dark depths of her eyes. Saving someone when she couldn't save her sister. Finding the monster who'd done this to our families. I reached across the table, the few inches that separated us, and covered her hand with mine. Then I began to tell her what I'd learned in the last couple hours, which, unfortunately, wasn't much.

RIKI

His voice trailed off as horror crossed his face. I felt a pang in my heart that combined sympathy for Jenson with the excruciating loss of my sister.

I finished his sentence, "Because of Cici." I saw him open his mouth, most likely to apologize, and stopped him. "You're trying to find him, aren't you? Your brother, I mean. Let me help." My voice almost broke on the last bit, myriad emotions churning within me.

The touch of hand on mine startled me enough to bring my attention fully to the young man next to me. I didn't pull away, the pleasant sensation of his fingers curled over mine a welcome relief from the constant pain of the past week.

"Because of the way the campsites had been torn apart, the cops thing it's an animal attack. That whatever it was took Alexei deeper into the woods, that there's no way he could've survived."

I swallowed hard, remembering what Detective Harrigan had told my mother the day they'd found Cici. Remembering that the funeral tomorrow had to be closed casket. Jenson's fingers tightened around mine, and I realized that he'd stopped talking. I looked up from the graffitied table to see Jenson's concerned expression.

"Sorry. I don't always think before I speak."

A lock of jet-black hair had fallen across Jenson's forehead, and I felt the sudden compulsion to brush it back. I fought it back, but did lean toward him. "You don't think it was an animal though, do you?"

Jenson shook his head. "It seems too...organized. But I don't know what sort of person could do...that..." His voice trailed off, and I knew he was thinking about what we'd seen at the site.

"So where do we start?"

Jenson pulled a folded paper from his pocket and spread it on the table. It was a map of the area, specifically the forest where this had all started. I studied it for a moment, something about the rivers and treeline tugging at my mind. I pushed the thought back, and tried to focus on what Jenson had offered. A chance for redemption as well as vengeance.

A touch on my cheek startled me. I looked over and found myself staring into a pair of ice gray eyes.

"Have we met before this?" he asked. "I have the strangest feeling that I know you, but I don't think I'd ever seen you before..."

I shook my head, breaking the spell. "I don't think so either. We don't go to the same school."

And we didn't hang out around the same people. I didn't say that though because I didn't want to sound like I thought he was a snob or anything like that. We just didn't run in the same circles.

He dropped his hand, his eyes sliding away from me. "Must just be everything we went through together."

I reached out and took his hand, hoping he'd look at me again. "It's not just you. There's...I don't know...something." I frowned. "I can't put my finger on it."

He sighed and released my hand. He stood, pacing from one side of the small area to the other. "That's exactly it. It's like how there's something on the tip of your tongue, and you can't figure out how to say it."

"I've felt like that ever since..." My voice trailed off, but when his eyes met mine, I knew he understood everything I couldn't find the words to say.

He came back towards me, and I turned to look at the map again. He didn't sit, but rather stood over me, leaning down so that he could look with me. A comfortable silence fell between us. I ran my finger across the map, tracing the route that Cici and I had taken on that camping trip. I'd wanted to get her away from Mom, away from the drinking and Mom's latest boyfriend, even if it would only be for one night. I'd thought I was protecting her.

I bit my lips, holding in the sob that suddenly wanted to escape. I couldn't, however, stop the tears from coursing down my cheeks. My chest hurt as I held it in, but the pain wasn't anything new. I hadn't let myself lose control since it'd happened. I didn't deserve to grieve, didn't deserve the relief that could come with crying.

Then arms were around me. "I understand."

Those two words broke something inside me, and everything came flooding out.

Neither one of us spoke, but I didn't need him to say anything else. I knew he understood. Understood the grief. The frustration. The anger. Everything that everyone pretended they understood but couldn't. All of the reasons why no one had spoken to me, even looked at me, since that night.

It wasn't until my tears finally subsided that I realized I'd just soaked the shirt of a virtual stranger.

Heat flooded my face until I was sure I was as red as my hair. I pulled back and Jenson let me go. I didn't look at him as I sniffled and wiped the backs of my hands across my cheeks.

"Sorry," I muttered.

"You shouldn't be," he said, his voice soft. "I don't even want to think about how I'd feel..."

I raised my head, expecting his sentence to have trailed off because he was thinking about his brother. Instead, he was staring at me.

Or, more specifically, he was staring at my shoulder.

I shifted uncomfortably, turning so that I was facing him

square-on. "Something wrong?" I made my tone cold.

He shook his head and stood. Before I could process what he was doing, he'd grabbed the bottom of his t-shirt and pulled it over his head.

I stared for a minute because I couldn't figure out why this good-looking stranger had just taken off his shirt.

Then I was staring for a completely different reason.

Jenson's skin was etched with thin, white scars. They covered his chest, stomach, and as he turned, I saw them on his back too. It'd been hard to study them on my own back, but I'd seen enough to be able to spot the similarities.

"What happened?" I practically whispered the question, but it still sounded loud in the little room.

He turned back around and sat down across from me again. "I don't know."

I swallowed hard. "Yesterday morning?"

He nodded. "You too?"

I nodded this time. "I just woke up and there were all these...scars on my shoulders and back. No pain, just the marks, like something had happened to me years ago."

"Same for me." He gestured in my general direction. "Can I see the rest?"

I stood up and turned around, pulling my hair over my shoulders. "I don't have any on my stomach," I explained as I pulled up the back of my shirt. "Just my back."

I didn't hear him move, but I was suddenly aware that he was standing behind me. I felt his fingers ghosting over my skin and shivered at the almost-touch.

"I've seen this before." His voice was low, more like he was talking to himself than to me, but I spoke anyway.

"On your back?"

"No." He sounded puzzled. "What I can see of mine, they don't look like that. Not exactly anyway."

I tugged my shirt down and turned around to face him again.

"I have a photographic memory." He shrugged. "I used a mirror so I could see everything. There are similar patterns, but they're not identical."

I pushed back a few curls that had escaped my braid. "So we both have these mysterious marks that look like scars but aren't from any injuries we know of, and they just showed up on the same day."

"That pretty much sums it up, I think," Jenson said. "I haven't heard of anyone else with...these."

"Me either." I sat back down. I began to pick at a splinter coming out of the top of the table. "Was your birthday yesterday?"

I felt his surprise.

"No. November. I'll be eighteen."

So we were the same age, but didn't have the same birthday.

"Why?"

I looked up to see a curious expression on his face. "Because it was mine, and I didn't know if that was the trigger." I looked away when I realized he was still shirtless. "But if it wasn't, then that only leaves one possibility."

"That night," he finished my thought. "That's really the only thing that connects us. Five days after...you and I get these marks. The only two..."

Survivors, I thought the word, then tried not to laugh. I didn't know about Jenson, but I wasn't sure if I'd consider this surviving. I hated that word, even now more than before since I realized that the implication meant that Jenson's brother wasn't a survivor. That the boy was as dead as my sister.

I might not have known Jenson before today, but I'd never wish on anyone the pain of having lost a sibling. Well, maybe on the person who'd killed Cici, but there were a lot of horrible things I wanted to do to that person.

And I knew it was a person, no matter what the park rangers said. The cops were tending to lean toward the rangers' position, that the entire thing had been a pack of wild animals. The blood, the carnage...people were insisting that no human being could do that.

Except something in my gut told me that there was more to all of this than we could see.

"That night, I saw–" I hesitated, unsure if I wanted to say it. I'd told the police, but they hadn't even bothered to acknowledge it. I'd known better than to tell my mother. She'd have thought I was crazy.

Part of *me* thought I was crazy.

Jenson's eyes narrowed, and I felt like he was reading my thoughts as he stared at me. "What did you see?"

"A shadow," I said. I looked away, feeling the heat rising to my face. "Just before Cici...It grabbed her, okay? I heard the screams and woke up. She was looking at me. Then there was this shadow outside the tent and it...grabbed her. Pulled her right out of the tent."

"Pulled, not dragged."

I looked up when he spoke. He didn't sound like he was questioning me, just confirming what I'd said. I nodded. "It was standing up," I added. "Not on all fours." I scowled. "They probably think it was a bear."

"I saw the tracks," Jenson said. "They didn't look like any animal I've ever seen."

I raised my eyebrows, momentarily surprised out of my maudlin memories. "See a lot of animal tracks where you live?"

He gave me a quick grin that made my heart do a weird little skipping thing. "I was a Boy Scout for like ten years."

I'd spent the last week being ignored, and even before that, I'd been pretty much a loner. I was the weird kid with the non-existent father and drunk mother. I wore hand-me-downs and thrift store finds. I wasn't really picked on in school, but that was more because I'd always been invisible. I didn't mind though. I liked being alone. I hadn't found a single person besides my sister whose company I enjoyed as much as solitude.

Except I was starting to think that Jenson might be an exception to that rule.

"So you believe me?" I asked.

He nodded. "I'm not sure what it was, but I don't think it was a animal. Or even a pack." His eyes widened suddenly. "Tracks!"

I gave him a puzzled look and waited for an explanation. Instead, he stepped around me and I watched him go. What in the world...? I started to follow him, but was stopped as I nearly ran straight into him.

"Sorry," he said as he grabbed my shoulders, steadying me. "I needed to get something."

He slid one arm around me and guided me back to the table. It wasn't until we reached it that I finally saw what he'd gone out to get.

A different map, bigger than the one he had before.

"I don't understand." I looked up at him.

He unfolded the map and spread it across the table. As he smoothed it down, I saw that he didn't have it open on the city. Instead, it was open to the forest where we'd all been. He pointed to a familiar spot.

"We were there."

I nodded and followed his finger as he ran it across the map. He didn't say anything, but after a few seconds, he didn't need to. I saw it now. Saw the pattern that he'd recognized. I didn't have a photographic memory, but I recognized patterns well enough, and I'd seen this pattern before. Except not on paper, but on skin. On Jenson's skin.

"You see it too, right?" Jenson asked, his voice low, as if someone was going to sneak over to this part of the library to hear the two of us talking. "This is the pattern right along my spine, isn't it?"

"I think so." I straightened, my eyes automatically going to his back.

Without a word, he pulled his shirt off again and turned so that I could look back and forth between his back and the map. Now that I'd seen it, I couldn't unsee it, whether it was real or not.

The marks on Jenson's back matched most of the marks on the map.

Even though we'd said it, that the one thing that linked the two of us was what had happened in that woods, a part of me hadn't wanted to believe that our scars were actually linked, that they were anything more than some freaky coincidence.

This said they weren't.

"We need to get these on paper." I started to reach toward his back, then stopped myself. "We need to see them side by side."

JENSON

If I'd thought taking off my shirt in front of a virtual stranger was awkward, it was nothing compared to having her trying to trace lines on paper she was holding against my chest. Even before we'd moved here, I hadn't spent a lot of time dating or even socializing with people my own age. I'd gone on a couple dates, but that'd been about it. Riki was cute, and she was definitely the sort of girl I would've wanted to ask out...but things being as they were...

I forced my thoughts back to the problem at hand. Getting our scars drawn out onto paper so we could overlay them onto the map and see what in the world was going on here.

"Almost done," she said, breaking the silence.

I wanted to ask her questions, find out more about her. She intrigued me, and not just because we shared these weird scars. She didn't seem like she was much in the mood to talk though. I couldn't really blame her. I was grateful for a distraction from everything that had been going on, but just because I wanted one didn't mean she did. She'd lost her sister in a brutal manner. I didn't know how to deal with that.

I didn't want to know.

"All right," she said as she removed the paper and laid it on the table with the others.

"My turn." I lifted up a sheet of paper. She didn't look at me as she pulled up the back of her shirt. I was glad she couldn't see me since my hands actually shaking a bit before I managed to pull it together. I put it on her back and started to trace.

It didn't take me as long as it had her, and it wasn't only because I was bigger. She'd had to go around my sides and over my stomach and chest as well as my back, while she just had the scars on her back and up her shoulders. It took me two sheets to finish it. There were ten of mine.

Once I finished, I put those papers on the table as well and the two of us stood over them, comparing what we'd traced to the map I'd gotten. I reached for one of the pieces she'd traced of mine and held it over the map, looking for the match point.

"There." She pointed.

I settled the paper over the map, lining things up. After we got the first one, we knew what we were looking for and started to set down each paper in the place that fit. And then I saw something else.

"What's that?" I asked, my eyes narrowing.

"What?"

"That." I put my finger down and ran it along a line that didn't match anything. "It starts at the camp site and goes off to the west."

Riki straightened, a serious expression on her face. "Okay, we have mysterious scars that just so happen to match a map of the area where..." She swallowed hard.

I wasn't going to make her finish that sentence.

"Scars that match everything except that line," I said.

She was quiet for a moment, and then she said what we

were both thinking.

"I think we're supposed to follow it."

RIKI

I didn't want to say it, but I knew he was thinking it too. There was only one reason for us to have an extra line on the map that had mysteriously appeared on our bodies. I'd always believed in God, but I'd never had a lot of schooling on the matter. I didn't even know if He'd do something like this, but whoever had given us this map, they wanted us to follow that line. And, in my gut, I knew that would lead us to Alexei...and the monster who'd killed Cici and the other people at the campsite.

His face was expressionless as he looked at me for nearly a full minute, then he spoke, "I'm in."

I nodded, a sense of relief going through me when I knew for sure that I wouldn't have to be doing this alone. I would've if I had to, but having Jenson with me would make things so much better. I wouldn't say easier because I knew that none of this was going to be easy. If whoever – whatever – had taken Alexei hadn't killed him, it had to be keeping for some reason. And I doubted it'd be easy to get him back.

"What do we do?" I asked. "I mean, how to do we do this?"

He leaned back on the table, putting him closer to my height. "Part of me wants to head out there right now," he admitted. Then he sighed. "But we need to be smart."

I could feel the tension radiating off of him and reached out to put my hand on his shoulder. I'd been touching him when I'd been drawing the map, but this was different. This was my turn to offer comfort.

"We'll need supplies," he said. "Flashlights, foot, water."

I squeezed his shoulder. "We can get all that."

He put his hand over mine. "I'll get as much together as I

can and head up there right away. You can come up tomorrow, follow along the trail as back-up."

I frowned. "Why wouldn't we go together?"

He pulled our hands down between us and threaded his fingers between mine. His expression gentled. "Your sister's funeral is tomorrow, and I can't wait that long to get started. Every minute that goes by..." His voice trailed off.

At least he wasn't saying it was too dangerous. I gave him a sad smile. "I've already said my good-byes."

"You can't miss it," he said. "Your mom—"

"Will be too plastered to know who's there and who isn't," I interrupted, making my voice as hard as possible. "The marks showed up on both of us. We have to do this together."

I could see the war on his face as he debated between arguing with me and wanting me to go with him. Then he nodded. I leaned forward and gave him a hug. I wasn't usually a huggy person, but I knew he needed it. I did, too. It didn't last long before I pulled back.

"Let's get started," I said.

****

I hadn't realized how long we'd been in the library until I stepped out into the muggy August evening. Jenson and I parted ways at the entrance, neither one of us saying anything. There wasn't anything to say really. We knew what we were going to do. We just had to do it now.

I had my own list of things to get, and I focused on that instead of actually thinking about what Jenson and I were going to do. I hadn't been back to the forest since it'd happened, and going back there at night wasn't anything I was looking forward to. I was with Jenson though. Every moment we waited was that much less time Alexei had.

Mom was passed out on the couch when I slipped inside, a couple of empty glass bottles scattered on the ground next to her. I didn't even pause as I walked by. She wouldn't know if I stopped, and I couldn't let myself feel any sort of guilt about leaving her. I'd meant what I'd said to Jenson about my mother being too drunk to notice whether or not I was there tomorrow.

But that didn't mean I wouldn't feel guilty about her being there by herself. Even before Cici had been killed, I'd taken care of Mom. She'd never been any good at doing it herself. Sometimes, I'd thought about how that really shouldn't have been my responsibility, but I'd done it anyway. Now though, I had someone else who needed my help more.

I changed into jeans even though I knew I'd be hot, then my hiking boots. I tied a jacket around my waist, then grabbed my school bag from the closet where I'd tossed it in June. I dumped my books out and looked at my list.

It took me nearly a quarter of an hour to find everything I needed, plus a couple extra bottles of water from the fridge. This time, I did pause next to the couch. I considered saying something as I looked down at my mom, but the words wouldn't come. After a few seconds, I moved on.

Jenson was already waiting at the end of my street. His car wasn't expensive, but it was a lot nicer than anything I could hope to drive. I remembered having read somewhere that his father was some sort of wealthy businessman. Not like millionaire rich or anything like that, but a little more than comfortable. Yet another difference that should've put distance between us.

I got into the passenger's side and gave him a tight smile. He nodded at me before starting down the street. It was strange, I thought, that I could feel so comfortable sitting in silence with someone I didn't know. Except he did know me. Better than anyone else ever could.

JENSON
Gravel crunched under the tires as I pulled into the campsite parking lot. The sun was already down, but there

were a few lights illuminating the area and I parked under one. There were plenty of camp sites nearby, just a few feet into the trees, close enough to the showers and bathrooms that families who wanted the whole 'camping experience' could get it, but not be too far from relative civilization. There were other marked sites higher up in the mountains for the more extreme outdoor enthusiasts. The place where we'd been was about half-way between, so Riki and I had a bit of a hike ahead of us.

Despite the fact that the August weather was still nice enough, the parking lot was practically empty. Usually, this time of year, people had to book their campsites weeks in advance. The cops had cleared the lower campsites almost immediately, but it looked like people didn't want to take a chance. Where we'd camped before was still supposed to be off-limits.

When we got out of the car, I pulled my bag over my shoulder and pulled out the map we'd made. I spread it on the hood of the car and waited for Riki to walk around to my side. It was strange, I thought, how natural it seemed having her there next to me. Like we were partners in something, not just two people thrown together by tragic circumstances.

"We're here." I put my finger on a section that was somewhere around my right shoulder-blade. "The campsite is here." I'd traced that section near the base of Riki's spine.

"And the extra line takes us here." Riki indicated a place that had appeared over my heart.

The symbolism of it wasn't lost on me. In fact, that was pretty much all I had going for me at the moment, the hope that it wasn't just some sort of weird coincidence. The hope that it was actually symbolic, that I would find Alexei at the end of that line.

"We could go this way," I said, running my finger in a straight line from where we were to where we wanted to be.

She shook her head. "I don't think that's a good idea. These scars showed up for a reason, and I think we should follow it exactly."

I considered arguing with her, but something in my gut said that she was right. "All right." I looked down at her as I folded up the map. I held out my hand, needing the contact as much as I was sure she did. She hesitated for a moment, then took my hand. Our flashlights went in our free hands, and we walked together to the trail. There was something comforting about the fact that we were walking side-by-side, rather than one of us leading.

Neither of us spoke, but the forest around us was far from silent. I could hear all of the nocturnal creatures scurrying around in the underbrush. The mosquitoes whined and buzzed, but my repellent seemed to be working well because they left me alone. We didn't make much noise ourselves, which was good, I supposed. While, in theory, we had aways to go before we risked running into whoever or whatever took Alexei, there was always the chance it would come further down the path.

I lost track of time as I focused on the path in front of me. Riki's hand was a solid comfort, keeping me tethered when a part of me felt like it was getting lost. I didn't know if it was the fact that we were walking in the dark or the knowledge that whatever was going on was something far bigger than both of us, but everything just felt so surreal.

Her hand tightened around mine as we stepped out of the trees and onto the edge of the clearing. I could see the tatters of the police tape fluttering around, but most of the clearing was hidden in shadows. That was good. I wasn't sure what the clean-up procedure was for outdoor crime scenes, but I didn't want to find out. Apparently Riki didn't either as she didn't even pause, tugging on my hand to keep me moving.

We made our way around the edge, following the unseen path that our scars had marked out. This was where things were going to get weird. We weren't going to be anywhere familiar, and I wasn't even sure the line we were taking was going to be on a path.

"The two rocks over there," Riki whispered.

No one was around to hear us, but I was glad she'd kept her voice down. Even the animals seemed to feel that quiet was needed, because as we made our way over to the rocks, they grew quieter and quieter, until the sounds vanished altogether. It wasn't until we'd gone a few more steps that I realized it was dead silent, and that it'd happened the moment we'd stepped between the rocks.

RIKI

I was trying really hard not to let Jenson see how nervous I was. I'd had a knot in my stomach for the last hour or so, ever since we'd moved past the place where it'd happened. The forest around us was eerily silent, so much so that I could hear the two of us breathing.

As the night wore on, every so often, we'd stop to check the map and make sure were were going the right way. We drank water if we were thirsty, snacked on something if we were hungry, but we didn't talk. Before we started walking, every time, we would join hands. Any other time, the idea of walking through the woods, hand-in-hand with a handsome boy, would've had me freaking out. At the moment, however, holding Jenson's hand was the least of the things on my mind.

The world took on a surreal quality as the sky began to lighten. We'd walked so long that I couldn't really feel my legs anymore. I'd gone beyond the burn of muscles, or the pain in my feet, to that place where I was almost numb. I had no clue how far we'd walked, but I knew we were higher up the mountain than I'd ever been before.

I was moving on automatic pilot and nearly tripped when Jenson stopped suddenly. I jerked my head up, and realized that it was light enough for me to see the outline of something between the trees. I looked up at Jenson and he put a finger to his lips.

Well, duh. I wasn't an idiot.

I didn't even bother to glare at him though. There were more important things to worry about.

We were here.

I could feel it.

And I really wished I couldn't.

I had no clue what was in that cabin, but whatever it was, I didn't like it. The feeling was nearly impossible to describe. It was like drowning in tar or being suffocated by a nightmare. Something dark and disturbing and utterly terrifying.

Some primitive part of me – the part where fight and flight fought – wanted me to run back down the mountain. But there was another part of me, the part that had been angry from the moment Cici had disappeared, that wanted to fight. I didn't know what that would mean, and I wasn't sure I would make it out alive, but I was going to work my hardest to make sure Jenson and his brother got home.

I slipped my bag off my shoulder and set it on the ground. Jenson did the same, and then pulled out a long hunting knife. I went into my bag for the hatchet I'd brought from home. I'd gotten it for when I went camping, but I wouldn't hesitate to use it if I was threatened. Or, at least, I hoped I wouldn't.

I let Jenson go in front of me this time, and we made our way up to the cabin. It was still early enough that the air was chilly and fog still lingered on the ground. But the night sounds hadn't given way to morning ones. There were no birds, no animals. It was just us, and whatever was in that cabin.

And now I had a feeling that it was a what, not a who. And definitely not an animal. Every step closer, the sick feeling in my stomach grew, and it wasn't from nerves.

We crept up to the back of the cabin, and I kept an eye toward the front while Jenson peeked in through the window. I felt him tense a moment before he sucked in a sharp breath, but I didn't turn until he tapped my arm.

He put his mouth against my ear, speaking so softly that I

could still barely hear him. "One room. Bed under the window. Alexei's in it. Cabin's empty."

I didn't have to ask him to know what he wanted to do. It might've been a bad idea, but that was his brother in there. I'd do whatever he needed me to do.

"Look out?"

I nodded, understanding what he wanted. I followed him around the cabin, staying at the corner while he went on to the door.

Fear coated my tongue, and my heartbeat echoed in my ears. I was suddenly aware that I was alone out here, vulnerable. If someone or something approached, I might be able to get a warning off to Jenson, but that wouldn't necessarily save me.

It felt like an eternity passed before I heard the door open, and then I saw them come out.

Two of them.

JENSON

He was okay.

He was okay.

I kept repeating it over and over as I helped Alexei to the door. He was dazed, probably drugged, but I couldn't see any injuries. He'd recognized me when I'd woken him up, and he was walking on his own. Right now, that was all I cared about. We'd worry about the rest later.

Riki was there as soon as we stepped out of the cabin, and I could see the emotion in her eyes when she saw my brother, but we didn't have any time to talk or even enjoy the moment.

The silence around the cabin had broken, and something was coming toward us. Judging by the noise it was making, it was something big, and it was moving fast. I started to pick up Alexei when *it* broke through the treeline.

I felt my mind crack as it tried to process what it was

seeing. It wasn't human, but it wasn't animal either. It had fangs and claws, stood on two legs, and its eyes were two black, empty pits. Its flesh hung off its bones, rotting, the stench enough to make me gag.

"We can't outrun it," Riki said as she stepped in front of my brother and me. "But you two can...if I distract it."

"No." I shook my head. "I can't let you do that."

She glanced over her shoulder, freckles standing out starkly against her pale skin. "And I can't let another person die like my sister."

I had only a few seconds to make my decision. The thing was coming at us, and even though it'd slowed a bit, it would still be on us any moment.

I grabbed Alexei and ran.

I could feel the tears burning in my eyes as I left Riki behind, but I knew she'd made her choice, and I had to save my brother. The path that Riki and I had come up was directly behind the...creature, so going that way wasn't an option, but anywhere was better than here right now.

Alexei didn't make a sound, but I could feel his heart beating against my shoulder, and that was what mattered. A loud roar from behind me made my heart clench, knowing that Riki was facing off against that thing alone. I tried to force my legs to go faster, but I'd been walking all night and there was only so much a body could take.

I stumbled and my shoulder hit a tree. I pushed myself off and kept going. A few feet later and I wasn't so lucky. My toe caught on something and I flew forward. I managed to tuck Alexei into my chest and roll so that I landed on my side instead of on him. I bit back a scream as I heard my shoulder pop. The world grayed out and only thoughts of what would happen to my brother kept me from passing out.

Then I saw what had tripped me, and I did scream.

RIKI

"Great idea," I muttered as Jenson started running. I was glad he'd gone, glad that my stupidity was going to give him and his brother a head-start.

But I still wished I didn't have to face this thing alone.

I raised my little firewood hatchet and tried to figure out the best way use it. I knew I'd never kill whatever this thing was, probably wouldn't even wound it that badly, but if I could distract it, that might be enough.

Unfortunately, I didn't think I'd be able to do even that.

My fingers tightened around the wooden handle and I waited to die.

Then, suddenly, pain. Lightning fast, sharp slices across my arm.

I was too startled to scream, too startled to even think about how stupid it was for me to look down at my arm.

I stared. Red, angry scars were slashed across the underside of my arm, written in such a way that I thought they were letters, though not in a language I recognized.

Before I could spend too much time on what'd happened, however, the creature in front of me roared, and I jerked my head up in time to see it looming over me. It raised its arm, and on reflex, I swung my ax at it.

To my complete and utter shock, I hit it, and the thing jerked backwards, hissing and spitting as it tried to knock the hatchet free. It twisted and turned, slashing at its own arm with its claws.

What in the world had just happened?

"Riki!"

I turned to see Jenson running toward me. Even from the distance between us, I could see the red marks on his arm. Whatever had happened to me had happened to him too.

Again.

I watched in shock as he yanked his hunting knife out of his belt, and skidded to a stop next to me. In one smooth motion, he lifted his arm and threw the knife. It tumbled through the air, and I was sure it would miss, leaving the two of us defenseless.

Except it didn't miss.

Score one for the former Boy Scout.

The knife hit the creature with a meaty-sounding thud, blade buried completely in its chest. For a long moment, the creature swayed on its feet, and then it fell. Black ichor oozed out from its wounds, and it didn't move.

I looked over at Jenson, my eyes wide. "What just happened?"

There was a strange expression on his face as he turned toward me, and my stomach squirmed. He reached out and pushed back a couple curls that had fallen free of my braid. His fingers trailed down my cheek and I shivered.

What in the world was going on?

"Come on. Alexei's waiting." He took my hand and started back the way he'd come. He wasn't running, but we weren't moving slowly either.

"Jenson, what's going on?" My head was spinning. "How did we, I mean, you...and our arms?"

"You'll understand when we get there."

Well that wasn't ominous at all.

Alexei was sitting on a large rock several dozen yards away from the cabin, a dazed look still in his eyes. I wondered what had happened, but I knew it wasn't my place to ask. And then I saw someone standing behind Alexei and I stopped in my tracks.

"It's okay, Riki." Jenson's voice was strangely gentle.

"But–"

"It's okay," Jenson repeated as he slid his arm around my waist.

He led me around a couple large trees, and then stopped, looking at the ground. My gaze followed his and my legs gave out.

He caught me as the world went gray.

JENSON

I eased her onto the ground and knelt next to her. Air fluttered next to me, and I knew without looking up that he was next to us.

"You could have just told her," he said. "You didn't need to show her."

"Yes, I did," I said. I kept my eyes on her as I brushed my knuckles across her cheek. "She wouldn't have believed me. *I* barely believe it."

Riki suddenly jerked upright, eyes flying open. She looked at me, then to the right, then back to me. I could tell she wanted me to say that she'd been hallucinating. That she hadn't seen what she'd thought she'd seen.

Except I couldn't tell her any of that, because it wouldn't be true.

"Shh." I tightened my arm around her. "It's okay."

She stared at me. "Okay?" Her voice shook.

"Would you like me to explain?" His voice came form behind us.

She jerked, her head narrowly missing my chin. With a sigh, I helped her to her feet. She was going to want to be standing to meet him.

"My name is Viator," he said, his blue eyes bright. "And I was sent to...help you."

"Help us?"

He gestured toward her arm. The arm that bore the same new scars that mine did. "The name of God."

She looked up at me, the unspoken question in her eyes, and I nodded. I believed what he was saying.

"It gave you the power to defeat that demon."

"Demon," she repeated. "That's what that thing was?"

"Yes," he said. "And it was imperative that the boy live, so you had to defeat the demon."

"And you're..." Her voice trailed off.

"An angel," I supplied the word. "He's an angel."

She raised an eyebrow. "Oh."

I looked over at Viator. He'd already shared with me what I needed to know. "Will you make sure Alexei gets home?"

He nodded. "I'll stay with him." He glanced at Riki, and then back at me. "You both did well."

She leaned against me as he walked away. "I don't understand."

"I know." I led her back over to where I'd taken her before.

"I don't want to look." She pressed her face against my chest.

"I know." I kissed the top of her head. "And you don't have to. Just listen, okay?"

She nodded.

"God was giving us the chance to save Alexei," I said. "He sent Viator to give us the map."

She raised her head. "*Give* us the map?"

I shrugged. "I guess this was the only way he could do it."

She looked down.

RIKI

I didn't want to look again, but I forced myself to. It was the only way I knew to force myself into accepting what had happened, what was happening.

And there it was. They were. *I* was. *We* were.

Me and Jenson, laying there on the ground, face down, our backs all carved up. But there was no blood. Why would there be? They were dead.

We were dead.

"How long?" I asked quietly.

I hadn't wanted to see before, but now I couldn't look away.

"He said that we–we never made it home." Jenson's voice

was soft. "We ran after Alexei and Cici. The...demon killed us right here."

"So we never..."

"We never went home. Never talked to the police, or saw our families again. Not really." His arm tightened around me.

"We're dead." Saying it felt more weird than bad. Which was also weird.

"Yeah, we're dead."

His hand slid up my back to my neck, and I closed my eyes.

"I don't feel dead."

"I know," he said. "Viator said that God gave us the chance to save my brother, but that once Alexei was safe, our time would be up, and we'd...go."

I should've been afraid, I knew, but I wasn't. Once I'd accepted the truth, a kind of peace had settled over me. Everything was going to be okay.

I turned away from the bodies on the ground. That wasn't me, not anymore. What made me, well, me was right here, and it would be what went on. I looked up at Jenson and put my arms around his neck. His hands settled at the small of my back, and I leaned my head on his shoulder.

"You know," he said. "I really wish I would've met you before."

"You mean when we were alive?" I asked wryly.

"Yeah, then." He chuckled.

I felt the angel's presence before I saw him. Neither Jenson nor I moved to acknowledge his presence, but I got the impression he didn't care much.

"The boy is safe," Viator said.

I felt the last of the tension go out of Jenson, and I closed my eyes.

"It's time."

"We know," Jenson answered for both of us.

I felt the angel's hand on my shoulder and sensed the smile.

"Get ready," he said as the world disappeared in a burst of white. "Because this isn't the end. This is just the beginning."

Introduction to "The Collector"

This is based on a short story I found while cleaning out some old folders. I'd written the original back in junior high or high school, but the idea still seemed like a good one for a sort-of bizarre and creepy short story.

"The Collector"

Danny went skipping along the sidewalk path. Today was his favorite day because it was when everyone got to show what they'd collected over the week. Danny loved collections. He always did more than the teacher asked, but not because he needed the extra credit. His grades were fine.

No, he did the work because he was good at it. He wanted to be a professional collector when he grew up. They got to go after the big ones, the special cases, not just the ones who lived in the wild. Danny's uncle was a professional collector, and he'd shown Danny his lab once.

Suddenly, Danny froze mid-step. From the underbrush, he heard a faint rustle. It could be nothing, but Danny didn't think so. He had almost every one native to this area, and he wanted to show off a completed set one day. If he could get one of the brown ones, he'd be one step closer, and he'd have something new to show today.

"Danny! Get back in here! Your breakfast is getting cold!"

He heard his mother, but didn't move. She wasn't mad, so he still had some time. He had to catch one. She didn't understand why he liked collecting, but she liked when he had good grades, so she never told him that he couldn't do it.

There, a flash of color.

Danny pounced, letting his wings balance him as he snatched the creature up.

"Gotcha!" he proclaimed gleefully.

The creature struggled, swinging its little arms and legs, but it couldn't get free. Danny was too strong. He held the creature tightly as he hurried back to the house. He flew up the stairs, even as his mother yelled at him to quit playing around.

"Be right down!" he shouted.

He knelt on the floor next to the glass collection case and raised the lid. The liquid he sprayed in daily kept the collection perfectly preserved. He supposed they lived for a little while after he sprayed them. Sometimes, he saw their eyes moving back and forth, but they couldn't ever make anything else move, and that was what mattered.

He picked up a pin from his kit and put the creature in one of the few empty spots he had left. His face screwed up in concentration as he held the creature down with one hand. With the other, he positioned the pin over its chest. He had to try to get it right through the heart. It was the best way.

It made a funny sound when he shoved the pin into it. Sometimes he thought they were trying to communicate, but he knew that was just silly. Everyone knew they weren't intelligent enough to speak.

Danny picked up his spray bottle and dosed it with liberal

doses of the preservative. Pretty soon, the new one stopped squirming and Danny closed the case.

"Daniel! Get down here right now!"

Danny frowned. He still needed to label his find before school.

"Coming!"

Danny's feelers twitched as he grabbed his pen and scribbled down the right name: *homo sapien – classification brown.*

He affixed the label and gave his newest find a fond look. Only two more and he'd have a full set. Then maybe his uncle would take him human hunting in one of their more obscure habitats. He'd heard that some of them even lived in groups, similar to the colonies where Danny and the rest of his kind lived.

He smiled at the thought. As if humans could ever be anything like the great monarch butterfly.

Introduction to "Nightmare Class"

This is a short bit of free writing I did in high school after a particularly traumatic experience in biology class. Technically, it's flash fiction, not a short story, but it was never meant to be anything long.

When I was in school, animals that were going to be dissected were delivered already dead and preserved in formaldehyde. One day, however, a student brought crayfish in for our class to dissect. What he didn't tell anyone, including the teacher, was that they were still alive.

It was total chaos. While I had no problem dissecting already-dead animals, I wasn't happy when our teacher instructed us to kill the crayfish. I ended up having to ask one of my classmates to do it.

Several of us went to creative writing class after biology and, when our teacher gave us time to write, all of us ended up writing similar things. This was mine.

"Nightmare Class"

"Help! Help!" Jamie ran down the dark corridor toward the only unlocked door in the building. She could hear the clicking of their chitinous feet clicking on the tile floor.

They were coming after her.

Jamie reached the doors and slammed her body against them. They wouldn't open. Frantic, she pushed against the door with all her might. Still, it wouldn't budge.

She heard the laughing of the beasts behind her as they came to a halt. Taking a deep breath and swallowing a scream, she turned around.

They were hideous. Bulging black eyes stared at her coldly. Tails curled and uncurled, slapping against the floor. Two long antennas reached out, brushing her hair. In their long, arm-like pinchers was a sharp probe...pointed right at her head.

Introduction to Poems

When coming up with short stories for this collection, I decided to go through my old work – and I do mean old – to see if there was anything I wanted to use or rewrite, or something that would at least spark an idea.

To my surprise, one of the things I found were some old poems I'd written. Now, I've never considered myself even remotely good at poetry, but when I was in junior high and high school, I had one teacher who had us write in all sorts of creative forms. One of those was responsible for the following poems. I'm not even entirely sure what the prompts were, but I do remember that shapes were important as these poems were cut out into their own unique shapes.

While a lot of that is lost in the translation here, the poems themselves were, I thought, cute, and that maybe readers would get a kick out of seeing something I wrote at some point between seventh and twelfth grade.

"Shining No More"

Diamond star
Shining brightly above
White as a snowflake
  Down from the sky.
          Woosh!
  The bird falls
As snow in a blizzard.
The night sky
  Is thick with grief and sorrow.
For the star shines
  No more.

"Untitled"

HEY!
Don't keep me waiting
All day...
  Is there a bear
In there
Or not?

"Jealousy Is..."

Jealousy is a hummingbird
  That flits to and fro,
Poisoning people with its words
  Honey-sweet dripping sugar
Darting from flower to flower,
  Changing person to person.
Hate and anger raging
  Like nectar through a flower.
Jealousy is a hummingbird
  That flits to and fro

Introduction to "My Brother Versus the Squirrel"

Originally, the title came from these stories that my sister-in-law used to tell about this squirrel that was particularly vexing to my younger brother, and from time to time, we joked that I should make it into a children's book. Well, the children's book idea never came to fruition, but this one did take its place. My apologies to my sister-in-law for what I did. This probably isn't what she had in mind when she suggested I write a story.

"My Brother Versus the Squirrel"

My brother's gone missing and everybody thinks he's run away, but I know better.

It's all cuz of that dang squirrel.

It all started when my brother and me were sitting on the porch in a time-out because we'd been fighting. That wasn't nothing new. Mom was always putting us in time-out for one thing or another, but usually because we'd been fighting. This time, it was my brother's fault. I'd been just sitting there, minding my own business when he chucked a rock at my head. I hadn't been making no faces at him, no matter what he said.

So we were sitting there, and all of a sudden, this squirrel comes running up toward us. Now, this wasn't no ordinary brown squirrel, and it wasn't even one of those black ones they got in some places. This was a striped squirrel.

I know you probably don't believe me, but I swear it's true. This thing had black and brown stripes, and was twice the size of a normal squirrel. Most people might think I was mistaken and this was some other sort of rodent. Like a opossum or raccoon or something else. I had two people tell me I just saw a dog, but I know dogs, and this wasn't one. It was a squirrel. Swear on my life.

So it came running up to my brother and, of course, he

throws a rock at it. I don't know if he was thinking that it was going to attack him, or if he just wanted to be plain mean, but the result was the same. He threw a rock, and that crazy thing caught it and threw it right back!

Now, I don't know who taught that squirrel to throw, but it had better aim than my brother because it hit him right in the nose.

Of course, he started crying and making all kinds of noise. Mom shouted at us that we weren't supposed to be talking, and he told her that we weren't talking. He told her about what the squirrel did, but of course she didn't believe him. Who would? I mean, it was a squirrel.

She gave my brother ten more minutes in time-out, and then gave me the same, just for good measure. I told her it wasn't fair, and even my brother said I'd been good. Didn't make no difference. My brother had a big old bruise on his nose and I was the only one there, so it must've been me.

The next time the squirrel showed up, my brother and I were out raking leaves. It'd been two weeks since we'd first seen it, and I was starting to wonder if it'd even been real. Maybe I really had thrown that rock at my brother. It wouldn't have been the first time.

It was the last time I thought the squirrel wasn't real.

You see, my brother and I were raking leaves to earn

money for Christmas, and wouldn't you know it, that squirrel showed up again. It was up on a tree branch, chattering away like it was cussing us out or something. I ignored it – and boy was it hard to ignore something that big – but my brother just couldn't let it be. He had to start yelling back at it. And, sure enough, he got it mad. Every time he finished raking a spot under the tree, that dang squirrel went running up and down the branches, collecting leaves and throwing them down on the ground.

First, we tried to ignore it, figured it would have to run out of leaves at some point. But it just kept going until my head started to hurt. My brother got fed up first, of course. He threw his rake at the squirrel, but that rodent just ran up higher and laughed.

I kept working, but my brother started looking for rocks and nuts to throw. None of 'em got even close, and all that squirrel did was laugh and laugh. But when Mom came out to see what was going on, the squirrel was gone.

For the next three months, it kept happening. The squirrel would show up and do something to my brother, then leave before anyone else saw it. Broke our mom's favorite candy dish. Ate all of the banana nut bread Mom had made for Dad's birthday. Knocked over the bird feeder, and tormented the cat. It even scratched up Dad's new truck.

By the time my brother disappeared, he was grounded until he was eighty. No one ever believed him about that squirrel.

I guess I didn't help 'cuz after those first two times, I never told anybody that I'd seen the squirrel too. Everybody already thought my brother was crazy. I didn't need them thinking I was soft in the head too. Wouldn't do nobody any good 'cuz just me saying it hadn't made any difference that first time, and it sure wasn't going to make a difference now.

Besides, I never thought it'd go this far. Seemed to me that the squirrel just liked bugging my brother. And I couldn't blame it. I liked doing it too. True, it'd gone a bit far some times, but it was a squirrel. Couldn't expect it to know how to behave like a person.

But that last time, it went too far. Everybody knew my brother was in trouble a lot, and that our parents had told him if he did one more thing, they were going to ship him off to military school. See, that's why everybody thinks he ran away, 'cuz something happened one more time. I don't know if Mom and Dad were serious about sending him away, but people said my brother thought they were, since he left the night before they could do it.

What happened was this.

It was Christmas and we were having a big party. My brother was supposed to be up in his room, being punished for the rest of his life, but I saw him sneak down when everyone was in the living room talking. I knew he just wanted some cookies because I'd told him I'd bring him some. He must've wanted to get them for himself because I saw him tiptoeing into the kitchen.

Then we all heard a crash, then another, and a shout, and we all went running. There, in the middle of the kitchen was my brother, covered with punch. All the food was on the floor, ruined. The punch bowl that my Great-Aunt Ilda had given Mom and Dad for their wedding was in pieces. The sliding glass door was off its track, the screen ripped clean in two.

But that wasn't even the worst. The worst was when Mom and Dad saw little scraps of wrapping paper mixed in with all the other stuff and they went downstairs to the tree. All the presents had been torn apart. Not just the wrappings, but some of the gifts too. Dolls ruined. Blocks thrown all around. Clothes chewed up.

Mom and Dad were so many that they couldn't even talk. The party was over and everyone went home. My brother went to his room without even trying to explain, and I knew that meant it was that squirrel again. I tried to talk to him, 'cuz I knew this was bad, but he just shook his head and closed the door behind him.

The next morning, he was gone.

We looked everywhere for him, but all we saw were footprints heading off toward the woods. Well, that was all the adults saw. I saw the little marks in the snow that said my brother had been following something.

That squirrel.

We looked all morning before Mom and Dad called the police. Some clothes were missing and my brother's book bag. We couldn't tell if there was any food gone since everything was still sort of messy from the night before. The police were real nice, but I could tell they thought the same thing as my parents, that my brother had run away.

They searched the woods. Even called in some dogs to try to catch a scent. All that happened was they got to the same clearing where we'd followed the tracks and then stopped. The tracks disappeared. There was plenty of snow in front of them, but nothing.

They said my brother had probably just back-tracked and then gone to hitch a ride on the road. I tried telling them that he wasn't that smart, but Mom just told me to hush. No one wanted to hear about the other prints or that squirrel.

Posters went up and rewards got offered even though no one thought my brother had been kidnapped. Every time the phone rang, they thought it was him. But it never was. And I knew it never would be. He was gone, and that squirrel was the reason why.

Now, I know how crazy it sounds, saying a squirrel took my brother, but it's the truth. Cross my heart. You might be asking how in the world that could possibly happen. Well, I'll tell you.

It's 'cuz that squirrel wasn't a squirrel at all. It was something else. It was too smart to be just any old squirrel. So here's what I think. I think that squirrel was a scout, and it came here from somewhere else, and that it decided to take my brother back with it. I think he's on some space ship or other planet, and that squirrel is still laughing at him.

I know, it sounds crazy. Why do you think I didn't tell anyone all this before? I saw what happened to Uncle Louie when he started wearing that foil hat of his, and I didn't want to go that way.

Why did I decide to tell it now though, after all these years? Well, that's simple too.

You see, last night, I was standing at the window, looking out at the woods, and I saw it. A bright flash of light. And then, just a couple minutes later, there it was.

That dang squirrel.

It was back. And this time, it was my turn.

"A Letter for Jenny" Introduction

Suicide is an epidemic, and one that I've not only dealt with in my years working with youth, but also one that hit close to home when I was growing up. Depression isn't just something that people can shake off, or a teenager simply being moody. It is a real problem that needs to be addressed.

This short story was prompted by something that happened shortly after I graduated high school.

The poem preceding it wasn't written for this specific story, but when I read it, it made me think of "A Letter for Jenny," and the author granted permission for me to print it here as part of the introduction.

"Never Alone"

by Angela Owsley

Ppl say I'm complicated.
But that's just bc they don't wanna try.
Don't really notice me,
Till I say I wanna die.

I pretend I'm strong.
I try to carry on.
Listen to all their shit.
Even when I don't believe it.

Get mad bc I'm so closed off.
But why come to you?
You don't believe in
What I go through.

Every freakin day waking up to pain.
Have every single person, thinking I'm insane.

Don't know how to walk away,
from the storm that's in my brain.

If beauty's on the inside,
I'm screwed, bc I always want to cry.
Always want to hide.
Always want to die.

Hardest part about depression?
In ur head,
You always hear the voices saying yes.

"A Letter for Jenny"

Dear Jenny,

From the moment I entered the funeral hall that muggy summer afternoon, I knew I'd never forget your face again. You must have dyed your hair at some point because the light-colored strands lying around your tanned face weren't the deep brown I'd seen in the yearbook earlier that day.

According to your cousin, the long black gloves and elegant black dress you were wearing had been bought for a junior high dance that year. I wonder if you knew when you bought it that the next time you wore it...if you were planning all of this already.

Next to your casket was a picture of you and a young man at that dance. All these years later, I couldn't tell you what he looked like, the specifics of that picture, or any of the hundreds of others around the room. I couldn't tell you about any of the bouquets, only that the heavy smell hung thickly in the air, almost suffocating. But I can remember every detail about you.

The unnatural blond hair and fake-tanned skin. The silver tiara on your head, and matching silver necklace around your neck. The hands serenely folded across your chest. The look of inexplicable sadness on your face. So young. I couldn't sleep when I got home because every time I closed my eyes, I saw your face. I'll never be able to get that image out of my mind. You will be with me for the rest of my life.

It seems strange that out of your whole class, I was closer to many others, but it's you I'll remember you long after the others fade from my mind. Many of those I knew have already become shadows lurking in the corners of my memories.

After all, before I looked at my yearbook, I had no face to place with the name Emma told me. I hadn't connected you with the giggling little girl in the play I starred in junior year. I thought I had so much going on during that I never bothered to get to know you younger cast members. It wasn't out of spite; I just didn't think I had time. You were five years behind me in school, only there for a year and then gone. So many have passed through that school in the same way, I never stopped to consider that you might be different. I was too caught up in my own life.

When I heard, I couldn't cry. I didn't feel that I had the right. I didn't think I deserved to when I hadn't known you. Hadn't taken the time to know you. I can't help but feel that somehow I could have done something if I'd just taken the time one day to speak with you, to listen to you.

Would a word from a virtual stranger have changed

anything? I don't know. I'll never know. It's too late now to consider what might have been. But the might-have-beens are all you left us with.

Perhaps you wished for guilt and sadness to plague those you left behind. Perhaps you intended for your mother to find your body and be tormented by nightmares for the rest of her life. Did you intend for the same for those who had done nothing to harm you? Though I confess that we had done nothing to help you either. But did we deserve the guilt as well? Or were you so eaten up by bitterness that you didn't care?

By the way, your little sister, got to your room first. She'll never be free from the image with which you left her. That will be her last memory of you. It won't be of the times you spent talking until midnight about boys or even the arguments over clothes. It will be of you with that rope cutting into your throat.

Your friends, family, and some of those who didn't know you so well, all suffer from the guilt of not having done anything to stop you. Did you realize that when you pulled that noose tight, that you weren't ending anything? You merely started a new, horrific chapter in the lives of your loved ones. Ending your life didn't help anyone, not even yourself. You're lost forever and those of us left behind have to struggle on with the knowledge that we had done nothing to prevent it. Even after these years have passed, the knowledge still weighs heavy on my mind.

I know it's foolish to write to you. You'll never read this letter. You'll never read anything again. But, out there, maybe there's someone who needs to know that there are people who care. That someone loves them. Believe me, there is always someone. You must not have thought so. How could you have done this if you thought anyone cared? They did. You may have had to look, but I know there were people that loved you. They still do.

I know because I was there at the funeral parlor. I saw the tear-streaked faces of your friends. Held your cousin while her tears soaked my shirt. I listened while they all talked about the fun you used to have with them.

They related stories you had told. Stories they now saw you'd told to hide the truth. Several of them wondered out loud what kind of pain you must have been in to do this. What you must have been thinking when made the final decision to go through with it. They shed tears as they said they never knew that life had gotten that bad for you. Some speculated about rumors they'd heard about you, about your stepfather. Rumors that may have had more truth than falsehood to them. More than one said that if only they'd known, they would have done something to help you. Maybe knowing how much they cared would have made the difference. Maybe.

The guilt hasn't been limited to your friends only, though I have yet to hear your mother confess that her own neglect contributed to your death. Your friends and I watched in anger as the very same superintendent who'd ordered your removal from our school came to pay his condolences. None of us could believe that he dared appear at the funeral home. How could he act as if he'd cared for you at all. If you'd remained at our school, maybe one of the teachers or students could have done something to prevent this. I later realized that he had come out of guilt rather than true sympathy. His rejection of you was just one more thing to deal with, wasn't it? Especially since he was supposed to represent a God of unconditional love.

I'm back at the school now, almost ten years after I graduated. I'm teaching the same age you were, and I try let them know that I'm someone they can come to no matter how big their problem might seem.

Maybe I'll be the person who makes it through some of the walls they put up. Maybe I'll be the person who they can trust. I'm sorry that I wasn't that person for you. Maybe if I had been, you'd still be here.

Now it's too late. All I can do is try to keep other kids

from making the same mistake. Try to let them know that they aren't alone.

I never want to write one of these letters again.

Introduction to "Free"

While about a character in one of my novels, one doesn't necessarily have to have read them to enjoy the following short story, though it will make more sense.

This story came about when a friend of mine, to my surprise, fell in love with a minor character who, in my opinion, wasn't very lovable. While I didn't quite do as she asked, I did decide to write a little glimpse into the life of that character after the events that occur in my novel *Three, Two, One*.

Angela, this is for you.

"Free"

"We're not sure how much she can hear or see, let alone what she understands."

A man's voice, accompanied by footsteps. More than one set.

Heels.

A woman then.

Faint floral perfume.

Her nose twitched, as if some part of her still remembered that she was supposed to be allergic. She didn't sneeze though. She didn't know when she'd lost that ability.

"How long has she been like this?"

The woman's voice was familiar, but she couldn't say why. Another doctor? A nurse? Could've been an orderly. There had been dozens over the years. She'd out-lasted most of them.

"She took a turn for the worse last night. We had her family in earlier. It was her sister who gave us your name."

"Her family came?"

The stranger-not-stranger sounded surprised.

"How long have they been coming?"

"Several years now."

The man was the doctor, she remembered suddenly.

"You haven't been in touch in a while?"

"No. Not for years," the woman said. "We had a...falling out, and I didn't think she'd ever want to see me again."

"Well, her sister said she was asking for you. Said she needed to tell you that she was sorry."

Had she said that? Who could she have needed to apologize to that she hadn't already done so? Her mind had only been clear for a short time, but she'd tried to make the most of it, to make amends as best she could. Who was left?

"I'll leave you two alone," the doctor said. "Just press the call button if you need anything."

His heavy footsteps moved away, then faded altogether.

The scraping of a chair across tile. The slow, steady breathing of someone who wasn't quite sure what to do next.

Not that she could help there. She waited for some clue as to who her visitor was.

"Hi." The voice was little more than a whisper. "It's Jenifer. But I go by Jen now. Jen Stone."

Jenifer.

It took her fading mind a couple minutes to place the name, then the face. Both were more impressions than memories, lost in the haze of insanity that had been most of her life.

"I'm doing really well," Jen continued. "Went back to school and became a therapist. Got married a couple years ago. Widower with three kids. They're all grown, of course, but I love them like I'd raised them myself."

Slowly, pieces of the past floated forward and reminded her of why she'd needed Jenifer to come. Reminded her of how horrible she'd been to the sweet girl.

"I found peace," Jen said. "And love. When I left here, I met a woman named Angela who helped me. Took me to church. Told me about God and showed me His love."

She tried to move, tried to find a way to signal that she, too, had been able to come to that point. That she'd finally been able to think clearly enough to get what her sister and her niece had been saying all along.

Fingers wrapped around her hand and squeezed, but she couldn't squeeze back. She was getting so tired.

"I'm so glad you asked for me so I could tell you that I'm okay," Jen said. "And so I could tell you that I forgave you a long time ago, Noreen."

A knot in her chest eased as she let out a long sigh of relief.

A smile curved her lips.

Her chest didn't rise again.

Her eyes closed.

She could let go now.

She was free.

******

I jerked upright, heart pounding, skin slick with sweat. My breath came in heavy pants, like I'd just run a marathon instead of woken up at work where, apparently, the night shift had finally gotten to me.

"Are you okay?"

I looked up at the young woman standing next to me. Auburn hair, dark brown eyes, she looked enough like me for people to think that she was my daughter and not my niece.

"Weird dream," I said. I stood, gripping my desk for a moment as my head swam.

"You've been working too many nights, Aunt Noreen," Jessica said. "You really should let the younger nurses take those shifts."

I gave her a stern look. "Are you saying that I'm old?"

She grinned at me. "Never."

"Good," I said. "Because I can still run circles around you."

She laughed. "Not tonight. You need to go home and get ready to go back on the day shift. They'll need you sharp. There's a new batch of nurses coming in, and you know how it is the first day here."

I reached over and squeezed Jessica's shoulder. "That I do."

I didn't let her see the stiffness in my joints as I walked toward the break room to get my things. I wasn't young, but I refused to see myself as old either. Jessica's teasing didn't bother me though. What had thrown me, however, was that dream. It'd been nearly twenty-five years since I'd started working at Serenity Sanitarium, and this was the first time I'd ever dreamed about it. To make things even stranger, I'd dreamt that I was a patient.

And that I'd died.

I shook my head as I pulled my jacket on. Jessica's sister Nora would have some wonderful psychological reasoning for it, I was sure, but I didn't intend to tell her about it. I'd shake it off and not think about it again.

After all, it'd just been a dream.

Introduction to "The Do-Over"

While heading the drama team at my church, and as the drama teacher at Warren Christian School for several years, I often wrote the plays and skits we performed. Some of these plays were comedies, others were dramas. On occasion, I wrote parodies of popular movies and television shows, but the final play I wrote for WCS was an original. I had the last couple lines come to me first, and I'd even known which of my students I wanted to play the characters. This is was the result.

"The Do-Over"

Characters:
Margaret "Meg" Lawrence - middle-aged woman who wants a do-over for everything

Raelle Lawrence - Meg's daughter; Christian

Sera Abrams - Raelle's best friend; Christian

The Attendant – an unnamed woman dressed in scrubs

Franny Duncan - old woman; Christian; very funny

Iris Milton - old woman; Franny's best friend; Christian; very funny

Mazzie Greene - Franny's granddaughter; about five or younger

Rachel Hunter - college girl; Christian; waitress at the diner

Trina North - Rachel's friend; not a Christian; college girl; waitress at the diner

Skyler Wells – multi-colored hair, possible tattoos and / or piercings; wears jeans, maybe chains; Kindi's twin brother; Christian

Kindi Wells - twin sister of Skyler; multi-colored hair, possible tattoos and / or piercings; Christian

Kelsey Edwards - volunteer for Christian summer program for kids

Evie Hughes - volunteer for Christian summer program for kids; mom to Amber

Amber Hughes - Evie's bratty daughter who's being forced to volunteer over the summer

Isabella Tucker - Amber's friend; self-centered; popular

Tori Wilkes - Amber's friend; self-centered; popular

Prescott Channing - cranky old man

Clara Prince - homeless lady who's constantly being kicked out of the Café; has a stuffed animal she treats as a pet

Tristan Ross - manager of cafe

Donald Palmer - bus driver

River Clarkson – kid of any age or gender who is on the bus

Rylee Clarkson - kid of any age or gender who is on the bus
Gavin Reed - kid of any age who is on the bus
Nela Swanson - kid of any age who is on the bus
Lysette Flowers - kid of any age who is on the bus
Benjamin Singer - kid of any age who is on the bus
Mason Kane - kid of any age who is on the bus
Assistant Attendants #1 & #2 – can be male or female (though cast as one of each); wear scrubs and carry charts
Security Guards #1, #2 – can be male or female; dressed either in security uniforms or something similar

Setting:
Act 1 - café / restaurant; beginning of summer break
Act 2 - waiting room of an ER / doctor's office

<u>**Act 1**</u> - The Café

It's just before lunchtime, the first week of summer break. There are two tables at center stage and other tables scattered around the stage. It can be decorated as any sort of diner desired.

Already onstage are **Franny Duncan**, **Iris Milton** and **Mazzie Greene**. Franny and Iris are in their late 60s, early 70s. They're funny, sweet and a lot of fun. Mazzie is Franny's granddaughter and is no older than five or so. She's a bubbly, bouncy girl with too much energy.

All three are seated at one of the center tables.

Lights up.

Franny: So what're we going to order this morning, Iris? The usual black coffee and plain bagel or are we going to branch out to something with foam and more than ninety calories?

Iris (good-naturedly): You worry about your breakfast and I'll worry about mine. (muttering) Honestly, can't a woman eat in peace?

Mazzie: Grandma Bug, can I get a cookie?

Franny: Not for breakfast, Mazzie.

Mazzie: For lunch, then? I promise I'll be good. I'll sit still and everything.

Mazzie sits down and tries to sit still. It lasts about ten seconds before she jumps up again.

Iris: That's some little firecracker you've got there, Franny.

Mazzie (indignant): I'm not a firecracker, Ms. Iris. I'm a first grader.

Iris: That you are, dear. (closes the menu) I'm going to just get my usual.

Franny: Of course you are.

Enter (from kitchen) **Rachel Hunter**.

She's a waitress, working her way through college. She's a Christian but not obnoxious about it. She lives her life right and lets that be her witness.

Rachel: What can I get you ladies this morning?

Enter (from outside) **Meg Lawrence,** her daughter **Raelle Lawrence** and Raelle's best friend **Sera Abrams**.

Raelle & Sera are in their early teens, probably freshmen in high school. They're dressed simply, not too flashy or too conservative. Meg is very business-like and tough. The trio heads for a table near the center as Rachel takes orders from Franny, Iris & Mazzie.

Franny mouths the words with Iris as Iris orders.

Iris: Black coffee and a plain bagel (catches Franny & glares; Franny smiles innocently) with cream cheese on the side.

Franny (feigning shock): A change? Oh my. Are you sure you can handle the cream cheese on the side?

Rachel (amused by the exchange; to Franny): And for you?

Franny: Hm. How about some orange mango tea, chocolate chip pancakes with whipped cream and a side of bacon, nice and crisp.

Iris: And a heart attack on the side. Honestly, Franny, you should eat better.

Franny: Iris dear, the good Lord won't be taking me home 'til He's good and ready. Might as well enjoy the food He put here on earth.

Rachel (to Mazzie): What about you?

Mazzie: Chocolate chip pancakes with whipped cream and cocoa. (sneaks a glance at Franny, then whispers) And a cookie.

Franny: Mazzie.

Mazzie (pouts): Okay. No cookie. (beat) 'Til lunch.

Rachel: All right. I'll be back with your drinks in a minute.

As Rachel starts to head back to the kitchen, Meg calls for her.

Meg: Excuse me, can we get some service?

Rachel walks over to Meg, et al.

Rachel: What can I do for you?

Meg: I'd like a cup of coffee. Just bring out the sugar and cream. The girls will have milk.

Sera: Mrs. Lawrence, I can't drink milk.

Meg: Fine. (to Rachel) Water for her.

Rachel: I'll have your drinks for you in a few minutes.

Exit (to kitchen) Rachel.
Franny and Iris have been watching the exchange.

Franny: Nice lady.

Iris: I think that's Meg Lawrence.

Franny: Who?

Iris: She owns the flower shop on the corner of Newton and Chase.

Franny: Right.

Enter (from outside) **Skyler** and **Kindi Wells**.
The brother and sister pair are nothing like Raelle and Sera. They definitely march to their own drummer and don't really care what anyone else thinks about them. Their clothes and hairstyles reflect their individuality: tattoos, dyed hair, etc.

Enter **Trina North**.
Trina is about Rachel's age, also working her way through college. Unlike Rachel, Trina is not a Christian and doesn't really have much patience for faith. Even though she and Rachel are good friends, Trina often expresses her annoyance with religion and God.

Skyler and Kindi sit near Meg, Raelle and Sera. Meg doesn't look happy about this.

Trina goes over to Skyler & Kindi.

Trina: What can I get for you two?

Skyler: Mountain Dew, a double chocolate chip muffin, scrambled eggs and toast.

Trina: What would you like on your toast?

Skyler: Cranberry jelly if you've got it. And bring some extra for my eggs.

Trina: Seriously? (Skyler smiles; Trina shrugs) Okay. (to Kindi) What about you?

Kindi: Waffles with blueberries and a glass of milk.

Trina: You've got it.

Exit (to kitchen) Trina.
Enter (from kitchen) Rachel.
She carries a tray w/cups, etc and brings them to Franny, Iris & Mazzie. When she's done, she leaves.
Exit (to kitchen) Rachel.

Meg: So, Sera, did you get the grade for your history final?

Sera: Yeah, I got a ninety-two.

Meg: See, Raelle, Sera got a B.

Raelle: I got a B, too, Mom.

Meg: You got an eighty-six.

Raelle: That's a B.

Meg: But it's not a ninety-two.

Raelle: Let it go, Mom.

Meg: I still think you should talk to your teacher, take the test again.

Sera: It might be a little late for that, Mrs. Lawrence.

Meg: It's never too late. Besides, why else am I paying to send you to a private school? I should get my money's worth.

Enter (from kitchen) Rachel.
She brings the drinks to Meg, Sera and Raelle.

Rachel: Are you ready to order your food?

They nod & mime ordering as the next group enters. When finished, Rachel leaves.
Exit (to kitchen) Rachel.

Enter (from outside) **Kelsey Edwards**, **Evie Hughes** and her daughter **Amber Hughes**.
Kelsey and Evie are about the same age. Evie's nice enough, but a bit clueless about her daughter. Amber's a teenager and is not at all happy about being with her mother. They're talking as they find a seat.

Evie: How about some breakfast before we head to the school?

Amber: I still can't believe you're making me go to school during summer vacation.

Evie: It's for a good cause. (beat) Besides, it's not like you're actually going to be in class or anything.

Amber just scowls.

Kelsey: What are you going to be doing, Amber?\I

Amber: Who cares.

Evie: Amber's going to be looking after the younger kids during recreation time.

Amber: I hate little kids.

Kelsey: I'm sure you don't mean that.

Amber: Oh, I do.

Evie: What do you want for breakfast, sweetie?

Amber: Half a grapefruit and a health drink.

Evie: I don't think they have health drinks here.

Amber: Then why did you bring me here? You want me to get fat, don't you?

Evie: No, sweetie, that's not it at all. And you're not fat...

Amber: Just stop, Mom. Don't even bother trying.

Enter (from kitchen) Trina.
She takes food to Skyler & Kindi.

Amber (seeing where Trina went): You've got to be kidding me.

Evie: What is it, honey?

Amber: It's Skyler and Kindi Wells.

Kelsey: Who?

Amber (pointing): Kindi and Skyler Wells from school.
They're in my class, but Skyler's leaving to go to some music
school. They're serious goody-two-shoes.

Kelsey and Evie look at Skyler and Kindi, a bit confused by
Amber's comment.

Evie: Really?

Amber: Trust me. They're trying to start a Bible study at
school.

Kelsey: Isn't that a good thing?

Amber: Seriously?

Trina crosses to Kelsey, Evie and Amber.

Trina: What can I get you ladies this morning?

They mime ordering as the dialogue turns to other characters.
Enter (from kitchen) Rachel.
She makes sure Franny, Iris and Mazzie are doing okay.

Enter Prescott Channing.
He's a cranky old man, a regular customer who's never in a
pleasant mood. He sits right next to Kelsey, Evie and Amber,
obviously in Trina's section.

Meg (calling to Rachel): Excuse me, miss!

Rachel (crossing): Yes?

Meg: I've changed my mind. I want pancakes, not waffles.

Rachel: Oh, okay, I'll let the kitchen know.

She turns to walk away when Meg stops her again.

Meg: And no eggs.

Rachel: Sure.

Exit (to kitchen) Rachel.
Enter **The Attendant**, **Isabella Tucker** and **Tori Wilkes**.
The Attendant just slides into a nearby seat without saying
anything to anyone.
Isabella and Tori are Amber's best friends – almost clones.
It's a little unnerving. They immediately spot Amber and hurry
over.

Isabella: I thought you said you were busy today.

Amber: Unfortunately, that's true.

Evie: Amber, aren't you going to introduce us to your
friends?

Amber (annoyed): Mom, it's Isabella and Tori. You've met
them before.

Evie: Oh, right. Nice to see you again.

Kelsey: It's nice to meet you girls.

 Amber (to friends): Ignore them. (beat) Anyway, Mom's
making me work at this stupid summer program thing at

school.

Tori: That's awful.

Isabella: You poor thing.

Enter (from kitchen) Rachel.
Trina comes over to Rachel.

Trina: Rachel, can I talk to you for a moment?

Rachel: Sure.

They move away from the customers.

Trina: That cranky old man is back.

Trina points.

Rachel: Mr. Channing?

Trina: You have to wait on him.

Rachel: It's your table, Trina.

Trina: Yeah, I know, but I can't deal with him. You can. I mean, that's part of your whole religious thing, right?

Rachel: Trina, that's not what it's about.

Trina (dismissively): Yeah, yeah, you've told me before. But you're supposed to be all nice and everything, so could you please be nice and wait on him?

Rachel: All right, but you'll owe me.

Trina: Thank you so much!

Exit (to kitchen) Trina.
Rachel crosses to Prescott.

Rachel: Good morning, Mr. Channing.

Prescott: What's so good about it?

Rachel: What can I get you?

Prescott: Coffee – black – and a blueberry muffin.

Rachel: I'll be right back.

Prescott: And make sure the coffee's hot. I don't want any of the lukewarm stuff you tried to give me yesterday.

Rachel: Yes, sir.

Exit (to kitchen) Rachel.

Amber: Mom, I'm going outside with my friends.

Evie: Excuse me?

Isabella: Please, Mrs. Hughes.

Tori: We'll just hang around outside.

Amber: It's the least you can do since you're making me baby-sit brats all summer.

Evie: Oh, all right. Just don't go far and be ready to leave when Mrs. Edwards and I are finished.

Amber's out of her seat before her mom's done talking.

Tori: Thank you, Mrs. Hughes.

The girls are walking towards the exit but pause by Skyler and Kindi's table.

Amber: Hi, Kindi. Skyler.

Skyler: Good morning. How are you three doing?

Kindi: Hi. It's nice to see you.

Isabella: Sure it is.

Tori (clearly being sarcastic): Nice shoes.

Kindi: Thanks.

Amber: What are you two doing here? Shouldn't you be a church service or something?

Kindi: It's Monday morning.

Amber: Then isn't it time to pray? Maybe do a little Bible study? Preaching in the streets?

Skyler: Do you have a problem?

Amber (to Skyler): No, we're just saying hi to your sister. (to Kindi) Hi. (beat) And bye.

Isabella: Maybe we'll see you around.

Amber: Yeah, if we decide we want to be losers too.

Exit Amber, Isabella and Tori.
Enter (from kitchen) Rachel.
She takes a plate and cup of coffee to Prescott.

Skyler: Are you okay?

Kindi (upset but trying not to show it): Yeah.

Skyler: Don't listen to them. You know that you're who
God wants you to be, right?

Kindi: Right.

Skyler: Then don't let anyone change who you are.

Prescott (to Rachel): This coffee is horrible. I want a new
cup.

Rachel: Of course.

She turns to go when the door opens again.
Enter **Clara Prince**.
She's a crazy homeless lady with a stuffed animal, probably a
bird, but she refers to it as her parrot no matter what it is.

Clara (yelling back out the doors): Don't touch my parrot!
(turns back and walks into the café, petting the stuffed animal
and talking to herself) Mean girls. Tried to take my parrot.

Rachel: Clara, you can't be in here.

Clara (ignoring Rachel; talking to Prescott): Would you like
to talk to my parrot?

Prescott: Get away from me!

Rachel (taking Clara's arm): Clara, we've talked about this before, remember?

Enter (from kitchen) Trina.

Trina: Great. Just what we need. Crazy Clara.

Rachel: Trina, help me, please.

Trina (crossing to Clara): All right, let's go, you old bat.

Rachel: Trina.

Trina: What? It's not like she understands what I'm saying.

Clara: She understands. She doesn't comprehend.

Trina: Good. We've cleared that up.

Rachel: Clara, you have to leave.

Clara: But my parrot's thirsty.

Rachel: If I get some water, will you go back outside?

Clara thinks for a minute and then nods.
Exit (to the kitchen) Rachel.

Trina: Perfect, Rachel. You're going to give water to a stuffed animal.

Clara: It's a parrot.

Trina: Sure it is. (sees everyone staring) Okay, folks, show's over.

While Trina's attention is turned, Clara wanders over to Franny & Iris's table.

Clara: Would you like to see my parrot?

Mazzie: I would!!

Franny (to Clara): Hi there. What's your name?

Clara (looking at her parrot): Clara Prince.

Franny: It's nice to meet you, Miss Prince.

Iris (pointing at the parrot): Is this yours?

Clara: It's my parrot. His name is Rochester.

Iris: He's very... um... cute.

Clara: Thank you. (to Mazzie) Careful. He bites.

Enter Rachel.
She brings a cup of water to Clara.

Rachel: Here you are, Clara.

Clara: Thank you, Clara.

Rachel: No, you're Clara.

Clara: Right. (beat) Thank you.

Exit (outside) Clara.

Prescott: Excuse me, is someone going to bring me my coffee? And I want to see the manager about that crazy woman.

Rachel: Sorry, Mr. Channing, I'll get right on that.

Exit (to kitchen) Rachel.
Exit (to kitchen) Trina.

Franny: Well, that was exciting.

Iris: That poor woman. We should do something to help her.

Mazzie: And Rochester.

Franny: When we leave, we'll get some extra food for her... and Rochester.

Mazzie: Can I pick?

Franny: Sure, dear. Now, what was the last thing we read on Saturday?

Iris: We'd just finished Luke 16:1-18 and were getting ready to start the story of the Rich Man and Lazarus.

Franny: Right. (opens her Bible) "Jesus said, 'There was a certain rich man who was splendidly clothed and who lived each day in luxury. At his door lay a diseased beggar named Lazarus.'"

Enter (from kitchen) **Tristan Ross**.
Tristan is the manager of the café. He walks over to Prescott.
Enter (from kitchen) Rachel.
She follows Tristan and gives Prescott his coffee.

Tristan: Is there a problem?

Prescott: Yes. First of all, my coffee was awful. Second, you have some crazy homeless woman wandering in and out of your café.

Tristan (to Rachel): Clara was back?

Rachel: Trina and I took care of it, Mr. Ross. And I brought Mr. Channing another cup of coffee.

Prescott: You need to do something about that crazy lady before she drives away all of your customers.

Tristan: I'm sorry about that, Mr. Channing. It'll be taken care of.

Prescott: See that it is. Your food isn't worth these intolerable conditions. Especially when accosted by a woman with a grimy stuffed animal.

Tristan looks at Rachel.

Rachel: Don't ask.

Tristan: Well, Mr. Channing, to apologize for the inconveniences this morning, your coffee is on the house.

Prescott: It better be.

Tristan (beat): Have a nice day.

Prescott: I doubt it.

Tristan walks away from Prescott, but is paged by Meg. Exit (to kitchen) Rachel.

Meg: Excuse me, sir. Did you say you were the manager?

Tristan: Yes, ma'am. What can I do for you?

Meg: We'd like to change tables. (she points to Skyler & Kindi's table) We want that table.

Raelle: Mom, we're fine here.

Meg: Be quiet, Raelle.

Tristan: Didn't you choose this table when you came in?

Meg: Yes, but I've changed my mind.

Tristan: People are sitting there.

Meg: I know, but I was here first.

Tristan: Ma'am, I can't just ask paying customers to move.

Meg: Well, don't ask. Tell.

Tristan: Ma'am...

Meg (interrupting): Look at them and then look at me. Which customer deserves better service? A pair of tattooed freaks with Fruit Loops for hair or me?

Tristan (after a moment): I'll see what I can do.

Meg: That's what I thought.

Tristan walks off to one side, thinking.
At some point during this discussion, Mazzie has gotten bored with the Bible study and started to wander. She's reached

Skyler and Kindi.

Mazzie: Hi there!

Skyler: Hi. What's your name?

Mazzie: Mazzie Greene. I'm five and I just finished kindergarten.

Skyler: That's nice. And where are your parents?

Mazzie: Oh, they're at work. I'm here with Grandma Bug and her friend, Ms. Iris. (Mazzie points; then, to Kindi) I like your hair.

Kindi: Thanks.

Mazzie: Can I touch it?

Kindi: Um, sure.

Mazzie: Thanks. (she pokes Kindi's hair; beat) Tell me a story.

Kindi looks at Skyler who shrugs.

Kindi: Well, when I was your age I thought that leprechauns were Irish midgets that came out on St. Patrick Day's to steal your toys. And every time I saw fireflies on St. Patrick's Day, I thought that it was the leprechauns taking my stuff.

Mazzie: That's awesome!

Franny's realized that Mazzie's missing and spots her by the other table. She hurries over.

Franny: Mazzie, what have I told you about wandering off?

Mazzie: Sorry, Grandma Bug. I just got bored. Can I buy a leprechaun?

Franny (to Kindi and Skyler): I'm sorry. My friend and I just got caught up in our Bible study and we clean forgot about Mazzie.

Skyler: No problem. (beat) You said Bible study?

Franny: Yes.

Skyler: My sister and I are Christians too. (holds out a hand; Franny shakes it) Skyler Wells. This is Kindi.

Franny: It's always nice to meet fellow believers.

Tristan approaches.

Tristan (to Skyler): Excuse me. That woman (points) would like to know if you would switch tables with her.

Skyler (shrugs): Sure, I guess.

Tristan (relieved): Thank you.

Skyler and Kindi stand.

Kindi: It was nice to meet you, Mazzie.

Mazzie: You too!

Skyler (to Franny): Ma'am.

Skyler and Kindi cross to Meg's table as Meg and the girls get
up. They switch tables, taking their things with them.
Enter (from kitchen) Trina & Rachel.
Tristan walks over to them.

Trina: What's going on?

Tristan: Mrs. Lawrence wanted to switch tables.

Rachel: She chose that table.

Tristan: I know.

Trina: Typical. Peope are never happy with what they
have.

Tristan: Just come get me if anything else exciting happens.

Exit (to kitchen) Tristan & Rachel.
Franny & Iris cross to Skyler & Kindi's table.

Franny: You know, my friend Iris and I were just
wondering if you'd like to join us for Bible study.

Skyler: Sounds great.

Franny: Excellent. We always like to hear what young
people have to say. (to Trina) Excuse me, miss? May we put
these tables together?

Trina: For what?

Skyler: Bible study.

Trina: You? Seriously? I didn't think God approved of
dressing like that. Or the hair. Or the...

Iris (interrupting): People look at the outward appearance.
God looks at the heart.

The two groups push the tables together while talking.

Trina: That hasn't been my experience with Christians.
(beat) Except Rachel.

Iris: Then it seems to me that your problem isn't with God.
It's with those who choose not to follow the Lord's example.

Trina: I'll keep that in mind.

Exit Trina.
The others sit down.

Franny: We're looking at the story of the Rich Man and
Lazarus. You know it?

Mazzie: I know it!

Franny: Okay, dear. What's it about?

Mazzie: A man named Lazarus and a man named Rich
Man. They both die and Lazarus goes to heaven and Rich Man
goes to the bad place. Rich Man sees Lazarus and asks for
some water. But Lazarus can't cuz he's in heaven and Rich
Man isn't. Then Rich Man asks if he can go talk to his brothers
but he can't cuz once you're dead, you're dead.

Iris: That's pretty good, Mazzie.

Mazzie: Thank you, Ms. Iris. I practiced telling the story at
school. (beat) They didn't like it that much.

Iris: No, I suppose they wouldn't.

Enter (from outside) Amber, Isabella and Tori.
They go straight to Evie and Kelsey.

Amber: Mom, I need twenty dollars.

Evie: What for?

Amber: Does it matter? Just give me the money.

Kelsey: Amber, you can't talk to your mother like that.

Amber: Mind your own business.

Evie: Amber. That was rude. Apologize.

Amber (to Kelsey): Sorry. (to Evie) Now can I have my
money?

Evie (handing Amber a bill): We're almost done here, so
we'll probably be leaving in a few minutes.

Amber: I can hardly wait.

The girls start to walk away.

Tori: That was easy.

Amber: Told you.

Exit (outside) Amber, Isabella and Tori.

Raelle (looking at Evie and Kelsey): Isn't that Mrs.
Edwards and Mrs. Hughes from church?

Meg (glaring): Yes.

Sera: What's wrong, Mrs. Lawrence?

Meg: Kelsey Edwards took my place on the church board.

Raelle (to Sera): There was a vote and Mom lost.

Meg: I'm demanding a recount.

Raelle: They counted the ballots three times already.

Meg: I don't care. I should get a second chance.

Enter (from kitchen) Trina.
She crosses to Meg's new table.

Trina: Hi, I'm Trina. I'm your server now.

Meg: What happened to Rachel?

Trina: This is my section. When you moved, your section changed.

Meg: Oh, well I didn't think of that. (beat) It doesn't matter. I want a refill. Black coffee with sugar and cream on the side. I'll add it myself.

Trina (to the girls): And you two? (they shake their heads) Okay. I'll be right back.

Exit (to kitchen) Trina.
Enter (from kitchen) Rachel.
She goes over to Franny, Iris, Skyler, Kindi & Mazzie.

Rachel: Can I get anyone anything?

Iris: Could I have a refill on my coffee?

Rachel: Of course. (beat) What are you studying this morning?

Mazzie: Lazarus and Rich Man.

Rachel: One of my favorite stories. A lot of good lessons there. (to Iris) I'll be right back with your coffee.

Iris: Thank you, dear.

Franny: Okay, Skyler, Kindi, what are your thoughts on the story of Lazarus and the rich man?

Skyler: We don't get another chance. Once we're dead, we can't come back, even to warn people.

Kindi: Subtle, Skyler.

Skyler shrugs.

Franny: I like it. No sugar coating.

Mazzie: Sugar? Where?

Franny: Pay attention, Mazzie.

Mazzie: Sorry, Grandma Bug.

Franny: What do you think, Kindi?

Kindi: Well, I think it means we should make the most of our time, because we never know how much we have.

Iris: Exactly. We should be sure we live our lives so that we can go home at any moment.

Franny: Sounds like you kids are on the same page as us. (beat) You know, we should make sure to tell our loved ones about God, because we don't get another shot at it.

Skyler: That's what Kindi and I wanted to do at school. We tried to get a Bible study started, but the administration said no.

Franny: Don't give up. Sometimes you've just gotta be more stubborn than them.

Iris: But don't do anything rude or against the rules. Remember, God said to respect those in authority over you.

Franny: But that doesn't mean you stop trying. Maybe you just need to be a bit creative about it. Advertise at school but don't hold the meetings there. Find a teacher who's willing to stand by you.

Skyler: That might work. (looks at Kindi) Those are some things you can try next year.

Kindi: Alone?

Iris: You're never really alone, dear.

Kindi: I know. It just feels that way sometimes.

Mazzie: Here. (She hands Kindi her doll / teddy bear) Now you've always got a friend.

Kindi: Thank you.

Franny: That's very sweet, Mazzie.

Skyler: Kindi's right though. Sometimes it does feel like we're the only Christians at school.

Franny: Then let's pray that God brings some fresh blood into the place.

Iris: I'll start.

Franny, Iris, Skyler, Kindi & Mazzie all bow their heads. They stay in prayer until Clara runs in a bit later.
Enter (from kitchen) Trina.
She crosses to Meg, Raelle & Sera.

Trina: Here's your coffee, ma'am.

Meg: Thank you. (to girls) Did you two want anything else? (they shake their heads; to Trina) Then I'll want the check as soon as I'm done with my coffee.

Trina: Yes ma'am.

Enter (from kitchen) Rachel.
She takes the coffee over to Iris. When she sees that the group is praying, she just sets it down and quietly walks away.

Kelsey: So, Evie, what do you have planned for today?

Evie: Well, I'm working with some of the middle school kids and I'm thinking that today can mostly be introductions and group games. Maybe do some Bible stories next week. I want to ease them into it. What about you?

Kelsey: I'm going to do some introductions and games, but I want to get started on the spiritual stuff right away.

Evie: We already have praise and worship at the beginning and end of the day. If we try to force it, they'll just rebel.

Kelsey: But it's a Christian program.

Evie: I know, but you can't push.

Kelsey: Giving a Bible lesson isn't pushing.

Evie: Look, Kelsey, I've worked with teenagers for years and my daughter's a teenager. This is your first year and your kids are still in elementary school. Trust me on this. Kids at this age need gentleness and love.

Kelsey: Not to seem rude, but I don't think that's really working with your daughter.

Evie: Amber's just going through a tough transitional period. She'll be fine. She just needs to know that God loves her and I love her.

Kelsey: Maybe. But maybe she needs you to set down some rules.

Evie: All kids go through this stage. She'll eventually realize what she's missing and come back. Meanwhile, I just need to love her.

Kelsey: Ever hear of tough love?

Enter (from outside) Clara.
She's really upset and all eyes turn to her as she bursts inside.

Clara: Bus!! Bus!!

Prescott: You've got to be kidding me.

Exit (to outside) Prescott.
Enter (from kitchen) Tristan.

Clara: Big bus coming!

Tristan: Look, lady, I've told you before. You can't be in here. I'm going to call the cops.

Clara: But, bus!

Meg: What's she yelling about?

Tristan: Nothing. I'll take care of this.

Meg: Well, you'd better because I am not...

Lights out as there's a loud, crashing sound.
End Act 1.

Act 2 - The Waiting Room

The stage has changed. It now looks like an emergency room, with an exit on either side. On stage are **River & Rylee Clarkson, Gavin Reed, Nela Swanson, Lysette Flowers, Benjamin Singer** & **Mason Kane** – all kids who were on the bus. **Donald Palmer** is also on stage; he's the bus driver.

Standing at the right door are two security guards; one stands at the left door; the Attendant and the **Assistant Attendants**, are on stage, all wearing scrubs. The Attendant stands next to Donald. Also on stage are Meg, Raelle, Franny, Iris, Mazzie, Rachel and Trina. All of them look like they've been in a horrible accident, except for the security guards and the attendants.

The Assistants are doing paperwork until it's their turn to get a patient.
Lights up.

Donald (muttering to himself): What happened? Something...I don't remember.

Attendant: Sir, what's your name?

Donald: What happened?

Attendant (repeating): Sir, what's your name?

Donald: Donald Palmer. (beat) I'm the bus driver.

Meg: You were driving that bus?! You're the reason we're all here?!

Attendant: Ma'am, you need to calm down.

Meg: Do you know what he did?

Security Guard #1 crosses to Meg and the Attendant.

Security Guard #1: Is there a problem here?

Meg: This man is the reason we're all here! He crashed a bus into...

Donald: It's not my fault...

Attendant (interrupting): Both of you need to calm down. (they stop & look at her) You're scaring the kids. (beat; to SG #1) Thanks. I think they'll be okay now.

Security Guard #1 goes back to her post.

Attendant (cont; to Donald): Do you know what happened, Mr. Palmer?

Donald (shaking his head): I don't remember.

Attendant: That's okay. We'll get to you soon. Just stay right here.

Attendant turns away from Donald.

Meg (to Attendant): My daughter and I, we're next.

Attendant: Names?

Meg: Meg and Raelle Lawrence.

Attendant (looking at list): I'm sorry, ma'am. The next names I have are River and Rylee Clarkson.

River: That's us.

The Attendant crosses to River and Rylee. Assistant #1
follows.

Attendant: How are you girls doing?

Rylee: All right, I guess.

Attendant: Let's get you taken care of. (beat) River, you can
come with me. Rylee, you'll go with my assistant.

River: Can't I stay with my sister?

Attendant (looks at her list): I guess that would be okay.

River: Thank you.

The Attendant hands Assistant #1 a piece of paper and motions
towards the right door.

Attendant: Just follow her.

Rylee & River stand.

Rylee (to Attendant): Are we going to be okay?

Attendant (smiling): Everything's going to be fine.

Exit (to right) Assistant #1, Rylee & River.

Meg (angry): What about us? Why do they get to go...

Attendant (raising her voice; interrupting): If I could have
everyone's attention. (all eyes to her) This was a big accident...

Meg (interrupting; pointing at Donald): It's all *his* fault!

Franny (to Meg): Mrs. Lawrence, you should let her finish.

Meg glares at Franny but quiets.

Attendant: We have a lot of people waiting here. If everyone will please be patient, we'll get to you as soon as we possibly can.

Meg (muttering angrily): Sure you will.

Attendant (ignoring Meg; checking her list): Now, where is Gavin Reed?

Gavin: Right here.

The Attendant crosses to Gavin.

Attendant: I have a few questions for you.

Gavin: All right.

They talk; the Attendant is taking notes.

Assistant #2: Nela Swanson?

Nela: That's me.

Assistant #2 crosses to Nela and appears to be taking notes.

Franny (to Iris): Well, isn't this a pretty pickle.

Mazzie: I don't see any pickles.

Franny (chuckles): Of course not, sweetie. I just meant that today didn't turn out to be as simple as I'd planned.

Iris (looking around): Looks like we're better off than some folks.

Franny: That we are. (looking around) You don't happen to see that nice brother and sister pair we were talking to?

Iris (shaking her head): No. I've been looking for them, but nothing yet.

Mazzie: Is the parrot lady here?

Franny: I don't see her, Mazzie.

Mazzie: That's too bad. I wanted to see Rochester again.

Franny: Maybe some other time.

The Attendant escorts Gavin to the right hand door.
Exit the Attendant and Gavin.

Trina: Well, Rachel, looks like your God wasn't such a big help after all.

Rachel: Trina.

Trina: Look at us. He didn't do anything to stop that bus. Look at those kids. How can you believe in a loving God when stuff like this happens?

Rachel: We live in a world where accidents exist.

Trina: Yeah, well, who created that world, Rachel?

Rachel: He didn't want it to be this way. It's mankind's

fault that bad things exist.

Trina: Right. Because two people decided to eat some fruit, the rest of us have to suffer.

Rachel: I know it doesn't seem fair...

Trina (interrupting): You're right, Rachel. It's not fair.

Rachel: But He gave us a way out.

Trina: I don't want to hear it. (beat) You're my best friend, but, sometimes, I just don't understand you.

Assistant #2 escorts Nela Swanson to the right door.
Exit Assistant and Nela.
Enter the Attendant.

Donald (to Attendant): Miss, was anyone else brought in?

Attendant (checking her list): Well, aside from the four we've just taken back, and those out here waiting, we've seen three other children: Julia Drake, Caleb Singer and Samuel Marcus.

Raelle (overhearing; to Attendant): What about Sera Abrams? Is she on your list?

Attendant (checking her list; shakes her head): No, I'm sorry. She's not here.

Meg (trying to comfort her daughter): That's good, Raelle. That means she wasn't hurt badly enough to be brought in.

Raelle: Are you sure?

Meg: Of course. You'll see. Everything's going to be okay.

Enter (from side; not one of the two doors) Kindi.
The Attendant crosses to Kindi.

Attendant: It's okay, miss. Just have a seat. (leads Kindi to a chair next to Franny & Iris) What's your name?

Kindi: Kindi Wells. Is my brother Skyler here?

Attendant: I don't have his name on my list.

Iris: We haven't seen him, dear, but we'll keep looking.

Attendant (writing down the name): You just sit right here and I'll call you when it's your time.

Kindi: Thank you.

Attendant (to everyone): Lysette Flowers?

Lysette: Over here.

The Attendant crosses to Lysette.

Franny: How are you doing?

Kindi: I'll be better when I find Skyler.

Iris: I'm sure he'll be fine.

Mazzie: It'll all be okay. God'll take care of your brother.

Kindi (smiling): I know. Thanks.

Mazzie: You're welcome. (beat) Grandma Bug, do you

think they have any cookies?

Franny: Why don't we find you something to do?

Franny & Mazzie look around & find something for Mazzie to color on.
Enter Assistant #1.

Assistant #1: Benjamin Singer?

Benjamin: I'm Benjamin.

Assistant #1 crosses to Benjamin.

Attendant (to Lysette): I think that's all I need. Right this way.

The Attendant & Lysette walk towards the left door.

Lysette (hesitates at the door): I changed my mind. I don't think I want to go.

Attendant: But you have to. (points) Right through there.

Lysette: Are you sure?

Attendant (looking at her clipboard again): Yes. Just through that door.

Lysette hesitates again & SG #1 takes a step forward, as if to force her.

Lysette: All right, I'm going.

Exit (to the left) Lysette.
The Attendant turns back to the waiting room.

Attendant: Mason Kane?

Mason: That's me.

The Attendant crosses to Mason.

Assistant #1 (to Benjamin): This way.

Assistant #1 & Benjamin cross to the right door. Benjamin pauses.

Benjamin: What about my friend?

Assistant #1: What's the name?

Benjamin: Lysette Flowers.

Assistant #1 (checking her list): She's already been taken care of. Follow me.

Exit (to the right) Assistant #1 & Benjamin.

Attendant (to Mason): Are you ready?

Mason: Yes. Which way do I go?

Attendant: Follow me.

The Attendant & Mason cross to the right door.
Exit (to right) Attendant & Mason.
Enter (from "outside) Amber.
She doesn't look as cool and collected as before. In fact, she's almost frantic.

Amber: Mom? Mom? (spots Kindi & crosses over) Kindi,

have you seen my mother?

Kindi (shakes her head): I haven't. In fact, I've been looking for my brother. Have you seen him?

Amber (shakes her head; upset): No. (beat) Kindi, what am I going do if I can't find my mom?

Iris: You poor thing.

Franny: Ask one of the attendants. They have lists of everyone who's been in already.

Amber: Where are they?

Enter Attendant.

Franny (pointing): One's right there.

Attendant crosses to them.

Attendant: Can I help you?

Amber: I'm looking for my mom.

Attendant: Name?

Amber: Evie Hughes.

Attendant (looking at her list): She's already been taken back. She was one of the first to arrive.

Amber: Can I see her?

Attendant: Let me get your name and information first and I'll see what I can do.

Enter (from right) Assistant #2.
He looks at his list.

Amber: What about my friends? Tori Wilkes and Isabella Tucker?

Attendant (looking at her list): Neither girl's here. (beat) Now, I need your name.

Assistant #2: Donald Palmer.

Donald stands.
Assistant #2 crosses to Donald.

Meg (furious): That's not right! He's the reason we're all here and he gets to go back before my daughter? Before me? Everyone else deserves...

Attendant (quietly): It's not about what anyone deserves, Mrs. Lawrence.

Meg: It's not fair. I demand...

Security Guard #2 steps forward.

SG #2: Ma'am, you need to calm down.

Meg: Don't tell me what to do.

SG #1 & #3 step forward as well.

SG #3: We have to go by the list, ma'am.

SG #1: If you'll just calm down...

Meg (fuming but calmer): Fine. But I'm not happy about this. (beat) And I'm going to speak to your supervisor.

Security Guards return to their stations.

Assistant #2: Mr. Palmer, please come with me.

Assistant #2 & Donald cross to the left exit.

Assistant #2: Right through there.

Assistant #2 points & then turns to walk away.

Donald: Aren't you going to show me the way?

SG #1: Straight down the hall. You can't miss it.

Donald hesitates but then shrugs and walks forward.
Exit (to left) Donald.

Amber (to Attendant): And you'll let me know when I can see my mom?

Attendant: I'll call you when it's your turn.

Franny: Don't fret, dearie. I'm sure your mother's fine.

Mazzie: I'd give you my bear, but I don't got it anymore.

Amber (not quite sure how to respond): Thanks.

Kindi: Why don't you wait here with us?

Amber: Really?

Kindi: Yeah. No one should be alone right now.

Amber (quietly): Thank you.

The Attendant has crossed over to Raelle.

Attendant: Raelle Lawrence, it's your turn.

Meg: About time.

Meg & Raelle both stand.

Attendant: Sorry ma'am. Just Raelle for now.

Meg: But I'm her mother.

Raelle: It's okay, Mom. I'll be fine.

Attendant: It's policy, Mrs. Lawrence.

Meg: I don't care about your policy. She's my daughter.

Raelle: Mom, just wait for your turn. I'll be okay.

Meg: All right. (to Attendant) But that's one more thing I'm mentioning to your supervisor.

The Attendant doesn't answer Meg, just motions for Raelle to follow her. They cross to the right door.
Exit (to right) the Attendant & Raelle.

Trina: Rachel, can I ask you something?

Rachel: Of course.

Trina: Do you ever doubt God? Doubt that He exists? That He's going to take care of you? Doubt that He loves you?

Rachel: Everyone doubts, Trina. It's what you do with those doubts that matter.

Trina: You make it sound so simple.

Rachel: It's not. I mean, think of it like this. Our souls, the reality of who we are, aren't made for this world and a part of us is always a bit homesick, never really comfortable in this skin. We never truly belong.

Trina: But you know God exists, so you're not like the rest of us.

Rachel: I know, in my heart. I have faith that He does, but I haven't seen Him either. I'm not basing my faith on anything more than you have.

Trina: It's easy for you.

Rachel: No, it's not. I live in the same painful, violent world that you do. I just know that this isn't my home. But I have to wait for answers, just like everyone else. Wait for God – who I can't begin to understand – to show me what I'm supposed to do. Wait for Him to finally take me home.

Trina: Must be nice.

Rachel: What?

Trina: Knowing that you have a place to belong someday.

Rachel: God offers it to everyone. All you have to do is accept it.

Trina (softly): I can't.

Enter (from outside) Skyler.
He spots Kindi first.

Skyler: Kindi!

Kindi (jumping up): Skyler!

They hug.
Enter (from right) the Attendant.

Franny: Your sister's been sitting here with us, waiting for you. It's good to see you, kid.

Skyler: Thanks for looking out for her, Mrs. Duncan.

Franny: Happy to help.

Mazzie: Grandma Bug, who's Mrs. Duncan?

The Attendant crosses over to Skyler & Kindi.

Attendant: Kindi, I'm guessing that this is the brother you were looking for? (Kindi nods; to Skyler) Skyler Wells?

Skyler: That's me.

Attendant: I'll be back in a minute to get your information. (to Kindi) It's your turn.

Kindi: Can't I stay with Skyler for a minute?

Attendant: I'm sorry, but no. You're next on my list.

Skyler: It'll all work out, Kindi. We'll be together again in a little bit.

Kindi: Okay. (to Franny & Iris) Thank you, Mrs. Duncan, Mrs. Milton. I really appreciate you waiting with me. (to Mazzie) I hope I'll see you soon.

Mazzie: Bye, bye, funny-haired girl.

Kindi (to Skyler): Don't be too long.

Skyler: I won't.

Kindi (to Attendant): I'm ready.

Attendant: Right this way.

They cross to the right door.
Exit (right) the Attendant & Kindi.
Amber's been getting increasingly edgy. Now she gets up and starts pacing.

Franny: Ants in your pants?

Amber: What?

Franny: Just an expression. You can't seem to sit still.

Amber: Mind your own business. (Franny & Iris look a bit surprised.) Look, it's nice of you to baby-sit me, but I can take care of myself. All right? I can do this on my own.

Skyler: You don't have to, you know.

Amber: Oh, really? I should just give up my independence and everything I am to be one of your little song-singing, Bible-reading, prudish, boring robots?

Skyler: Do I look like a robot?

Amber: Give them time. You'll be in a suit and tie, condemning the rest of us before you realize what happened. Believe me. I know.

Iris (compassionately): What happened to make you hate Christians so much?

Amber: When your best friend starts labeling you a "poor lost soul in need of guidance" and then tells everyone every secret you ever trusted her with... (realizing that she's revealing too much) It doesn't matter.

Enter the Attendant.
She crosses to where Amber is still talking.

Amber (cont.): I live my life how I want. I decide what I do. And no old women, or goofy little kids, or social rejects are going to change me.

Attendant: Amber Hughes?

Amber: I can see my mom now?

Attendant: This way, please.

They start to walk towards the left door but partway there, Amber stops and looks back at Skyler, Franny and Iris.

Amber: It's my life.

She follows the Attendant to the door and goes through without another word.
Exit (to the left) Amber.

Iris: How sad.

Meg: What a brat. I'm just glad she's gone.

The Attendant comes back over to Franny, Iris, Skyler and Mazzie.
Enter Assistant #1.
She crosses to stand just behind the Attendant.

Attendant: Mazzie Greene?

Mazzie (jumping to her feet): Is it my turn?

Attendant: Yes, it is.

Mazzie: Will Grandma Bug and Ms. Iris be coming too?

Franny: Hush, Mazzie. You just do what the nice lady says and I'll see you in a little while.

Mazzie: Okay, Grandma Bug.

Mazzie hugs Franny & then hugs Iris. She waves at Skyler.

Attendant (to Assistant #1): Will you take her?

Assistant #1 nods.

Attendant (cont; to Mazzie): Go with her. (to Assistant) I'll be able to handle it from here. Go ahead and stay back there.

Assistant #1 and Mazzie walk towards the door on the right side.
Exit (to the right) Assistant #1 & Mazzie.
The Attendant talks to Skyler & writes down a few things.

Rachel: I feel bad for Mrs. Lawrence.

Trina: Who?

Rachel (pointing): She was here with her daughter but the girl went back a while ago. Now she's sitting there all by herself.

Trina: Isn't that the lady who kept complaining about everything? Wanted to change her order and her table?

Rachel: Yeah.

Trina: She's crabby. Let her sit alone.

Rachel: We should go sit with her.

Trina: Why, so she can complain some more?

Rachel: I'm going.

Trina: Suit yourself.

Rachel gets up and crosses to where Meg is sitting, alone.

Rachel: Mrs. Lawrence?

Meg: Yes?

Rachel: I don't know if you remember who I am...

Meg: The waitress. Yes, I know.

Rachel: Do you mind if I sit with you?

Meg: Why?

Rachel: You just looked like you could use a friend.

Meg shrugs and Rachel sits.

Attendant: All right, Skyler, why don't you come with me.

Meg: You have got to be kidding! (all eyes on Meg) He just got here.

Rachel: It's okay, Mrs. Lawrence.

Meg: No, it's not. The rest of us have been waiting much longer. I demand to see your list.

Attendant: That's not possible ma'am. It's confidential.

Meg: I want to speak to your supervisor immediately.

Attendant: I'll let him know.

Meg: You do that.

Attendant: Skyler. This way.

Skyler (to Franny & Iris): Thank you both. You gave me a lot of encouragement when I really needed it. You're real Godsends.

Iris: You've got a heart for the Lord, Skyler. A true blessing.

Franny: And your uniqueness is a gift. No one should tell you different.

Skyler: Thanks. (to Attendant) Okay.

Attendant: Follow me.

The Attendant and Skyler cross to the right door.
Exit (to the right) the Attendant & Skyler.

Franny: What a nice kid.

Iris: Yes he is. (beat) You think that hair color's natural?

Franny: Wasn't in my day, but it matched his shoes.

Iris: That it did.

Franny: Think I could find shoes to match my hair?

Iris: They don't make shoes that white.

Franny: We spend way too much time together.

Meg (to Franny & Iris): You two are crazy.

Franny: It's been said before.

Meg: You sit there with this boy who I wouldn't trust with
my dog, and you let him talk to your granddaughter.

Rachel: He's a Christian, Mrs. Lawrence.

Meg: Might try looking like one.

Enter (from the right) the Attendant.

Attendant: Rachel Hunter. (Rachel stands) Time for you.

Rachel (to Meg): You don't have to be alone, Mrs.

Lawrence.

Meg doesn't say anything.
Trina stands & the friends meet halfway.

Trina: I've got a bad feeling about this Rachel. Don't go.

Rachel: Don't be silly, Trina. I don't need to worry. I know where my future lies.

Trina: Please, Rachel.

Rachel: Just remember what I told you. (they hug; to Attendant) I'm ready to go.

The Attendant & Rachel cross to the right side.
Exit (to right) the Attendant & Rachel.

Franny: Well, looks like we're down to the last of us. Don't know about the rest of you, but I'm eager to get going. Never did like sitting still long.

Iris: Now we know where Mazzie gets it from.

Franny: Her mom was always like me. Quite the handful, Cassie was. Did I ever tell you about taking her to the zoo when she was five?

Iris: When she tried to free the bears?

Franny: She was seven that year and said that they were her teddy bear's cousins. Haven't been back to that zoo since. (beat) No, this was different. James and I decided to take the kids to see this new exhibit. We didn't know much about it and, turned out, that the zoo had decided to add some evolution theory to one of their presentations. James and I are sitting there, all worried about how we were going to explain this to our kids. They were all so young. The oldest ten, and Cassie was five. So, the lady's up there, talking away about how a bunch of dust exploded and became the universe when Cassie pipes up with this question. "Where'd the dust come from?" This poor lady stammered around for a bit. I don't think anyone had ever interrupted her before. And then Cassie proceeded to tell the whole audience the Creation story. I don't think any parent could've been prouder.

Silence for a moment.

Meg: I would've been mortified.

Franny: I was at first. All I could think about was what these people must've thought. Then I realized that my girl was doing what God told all of us to do. She was sharing the Gospel, right there at the zoo.

Enter (from right) the Attendant.
She looks very serious.

Attendant: Trina North.

Trina: It's Rachel, isn't it?

Attendant: Step over here, please.

Trina: Just tell me what happened.

The Attendant and Trina step close to the left door. They appear to be talking, but it's too quiet to hear what's being said. Trina starts shaking her head, as if in denial.

Attendant: I'm sorry.

Trina: No, no. It's not true.

It's apparent that she's getting very upset.

Attendant (to SG#1): Can you...?

Security Guard #1 nods and takes one of Trina's arms.
Exit (to left) SG #1 & Trina.
Just as Trina passes out of sight, she screams.
It's silent for a moment. Franny, Iris and Meg are all shaken by
what's happened.

Franny: That poor girl.

Iris: How awful.

The Attendant crosses to Franny and Iris.

Attendant: Iris Milton?

Iris: Is it my turn?

Attendant: Yes. Come with me.

Iris (smiling; to Franny): See you in a few. (to the
Attendant) Let's go.

The Attendant & Iris cross to the right.
Exit (to right) the Attendant & Iris.
Franny gets up and crosses to Meg, sitting next to the younger
woman.

Franny: Down to just the two of us. Nervous?

Meg (shaking her head): No. I'm fine.

Franny: Iris has been my best friend since first grade –
except for the incident with the gum, but that wasn't my fault.
We started going to church when we were twelve. Baptized
together at fourteen. Married just six months apart. Raised our
kids together.

Meg (interrupting): Not to be rude, but is there a point to
your story?

Franny: Just that, even though Iris and I have been through
pretty much everything together, I've always had one friend
better than her.

Meg: Let me guess. God.

Franny: It's not as cliché as it sounds. He really has been
there for me.

Meg: Look, I appreciate what you're doing and all, but I'm
not worried.

Enter (from right) the Attendant.
She stays next to the door.

Franny (seeing the Attendant): All right.

Attendant: Franny Duncan?

Franny: It's about time. (stands; happy) I've been waiting
for this.

Franny crosses to the Attendant, smiles at her and then goes
through the right door without another word.
Exit (to right) Franny.
The Attendant crosses to Meg, the last person on stage aside
from the two security guards.

Attendant: Meg Lawrence.

Meg: I'm the last one. Of course I'm Meg Lawrence.

Attendant: Come with me.

Meg (not moving): Did you speak to your supervisor?

Attendant: Yes, ma'am, I did.

Meg: And?

Attendant (hesitating): He said he doesn't know you.

Meg: Excuse me? After all the time I put in at church?
Paying for my daughter to go to that school?

Attendant: He said he doesn't know you.

Meg: Fine. Then I want another chance. I want a do-over.

Attendant: I'm sorry, ma'am. There are no do-overs in
death.

Lights out.
End Act 2.
End play.

The Dragon Three Introduction

Several years ago, while reading a certain series of books about a magical world hidden from the non-magical world, I had the thought "what if all the world was magical...and what if one person was born without magic?" From that came an idea for *Dragon Eyes*. Originally intended as a stand-alone novel, as I wrote, I realized that Brina Fine wasn't the only character with a story to tell. Her friends, Aidan and Thana, each had their own tale. So *Dragon Blood* and *Dragon Heart* were born. I'd originally intended to make them three separate books, but ultimately decided to put them together, with each character having their own section.

What follows is the Prologue and part of the first chapter of *The Dragon Three*, then a short story "So It Begins" which is also included in my previous short story collection, *This Weak & Idle Theme*. You don't need to have read *The Dragon Three* to read "So It Begins."

Prologue: Hope a Little Harder

For centuries, evil had slept deep under the earth. Now, it rumbled, eager to return and destroy. Only One could survive against it, but the ancient scholars who had held the necessary knowledge had all but disappeared. And should the One prevail, the battle would have only just begun, for the creature was the beginning, not the end. Little hope remained that anyone could find the secrets needed to save the world, much less interpret them, but little hope was better than none, for without hope, the world would be doomed.

Chapter One: Just Breathe

Brina Tri Fine was no ordinary girl, for Brina had a secret. It was this secret on which she dwelled, resting her forehead against the cool glass of the backseat window. The outside scenery flashed by as the vehicle sped past, fields of corn and wheat, grazing garflags and cows. Bright yellow sunflowers and purple masnaeds bobbed in the breeze side-by-side. The sweet-smelling nosidam tree was in full bloom, its red flowers in stark contrast to its pale blue leaves. All in all, it was a beautiful day, but Brina didn't register any of it. Her thoughts were already miles ahead, dreading what was to come. She'd begged her parents to drive her to school, wanting the time to prepare. Not that it would make much difference, she knew.

She was just putting off the inevitable.

Brina glanced at the reflection in the window, studying the solemn face looking back at her. It was a pretty face. Not extraordinary like her older sisters, Barika and Basha, but pretty enough for people to notice. Tendrils of dark red waves framed her heart-shaped face, and the rest of her hair hung down her back in a waist-length braid. She'd gotten her hair color from her father. The twins closest to her age, Bem and Bae, were also red-heads. The other four had their mother's blond hair. All of them had dark brown eyes – mother, father, six brothers and sisters. All except Brina. No one knew where her light violet eyes had come from; no one in either her mother's or father's families had eyes like hers. But, then again, no one in either family – no one in the whole world for that matter – was like Brina. She'd long since given up asking Elsali, the Creator, why she was different, and tried to focus on what she could do rather than what she couldn't. Unfortunately, school probably wasn't going to be one of those things.

"We'll be arriving shortly." Vani Fine's voice cut through Brina's thoughts.

"Thank you, Mother," Brina replied automatically.

Fifteen years younger than her closest sibling, Brina had been raised more like an only child than the youngest of a large family. Her parents had doted on her, or so it had seemed to the outside world. Brina had been kept at home for her first fifteen years, taught basics by tutors who believed her parents were schooling her in the magical arts when they got home from work, which was understandable when one considered her parents' skill.

Her father, Ziven Fine, was Principal of Audeamus Elementary School, the most elite elementary boarding school in all of Ortus. Most considered it the greatest one in the country, and all of the Fine kids, except Brina, had attended. Vani Issa-Fine had followed in her own father's footsteps, teaching botany at the Seriatim School of Higher Education. Seriatim was a good school, but not as good as the Audeamus School of Higher Education. Only the best of the best achieved acceptance and most of them were graduates of the Audeamus Elementary and Middle Schools. A few, like Brina, were accepted based on the exceptional talent of generations of family members. It was for this reason, and this reason alone, that Brina Fine was on her way to Audeamus.

"Are you wearing your uniform?"

"Yes, ma'am," Brina didn't add how her mother could have turned around and seen for herself that Brina had already fastened her dark blue summer cloak around her neck. Instead, Vani chose to ask and keep her eyes focused on the road ahead. Brina sighed. It wasn't like her parents were mean or cruel to her, they just didn't seem to know how to behave around their abnormal child. Sometimes, she even felt sorry for them. This wasn't one of those times. She had enough going on in her head without having to worry about how her parents were dealing with everything.

"And you have everything you need?" Vani continued.

Brina almost smirked, but managed to keep herself in check. "Yes, ma'am." She bit the inside of her cheek to refrain from making a snide comment. Sarcasm and a quirky sense of humor – often combined – were her go-to defense mechanisms, and she was definitely on the defensive at the moment, what with her certain doom looming ahead. At least, she thought, the required school uniform was simple enough. Modest clothing, sensible shoes and, for classes and formal occasions, dress cloaks. It was the only simple thing about this entire situation. From one of her side pockets, Brina withdrew a long, thin piece of wood. *Hemlock*, she thought with a wry smile. *There's irony for you.* She twirled the wood between her fingers.

"Brina, don't!" Vani had finally turned around. "You could..." Her voice trailed off as she realized what she'd been about to say.

"I could do what, Mom?" Brina's voice was soft. Her hand

stilled, gripping the wood with enough force to turn her knuckles white. "I could do what? Poke myself in the eye, because we all know that's about all the damage I can do with this."

Vani studied her daughter for a moment, a mixture of wariness and sorrow in her dark eyes. "You know I'd help you if I could," Vani almost whispered the words.

Brina felt a surge of guilt and reached out to touch her mother's arm. "I know, Mom."

"So It Begins"

When the Durand family went anywhere it was always a fiasco. Fourteen kids, half of them under the age of ten and most with more energy than any one person should have. Marcile Durand had her hands full. As she always did, she counted on her two oldest, fifteen and fourteen year-olds Robb and Jozy, to help. This trip to their favorite restaurant was no exception.

"Robb, make sure you keep Amber and Cheri close by. They've been running around every time we go some place public." Marcile instructed her eldest son as she handed each of the eleven year-old twins, Julie and Janet, one of the two year-old girls. Lawanda and Lacilla had just started walking and squirmed in their sisters' arms, eager to be down on their own. "And Jozy, don't let Dede and Monica cross the parking lot without holding your hands."

"Yes, Mama." Robb waited for his nine year-old sisters, Alexis and Sarah, to climb out of the magically extended interior of the family van. He then helped the six year-old twins out of their booster seats. Cheri grinned up at her brother, quite the feat since he was already over six feet tall. "Don't even think about it." She gave him a wide-eyed innocent look that he knew better than to trust.

"Ouch! Mama, Dede pulled my hair!" Jozy called out from the other side of the van.

"Man up," Robb called. "They ain't that big!" He winced as Amber kicked him in the shins and tried to run. He scooped her up under one arm and her twin under the other.

"*Mira!*" Jozy fell in step beside Robb. He gestured towards his hair. His normal mohawk had one section bent to the side. "*Mira!*" He repeated.

Robb's dark eyes sparkled. "Jozy, you need to stand up for yourself. Can't keep letting the little ones get the best of you."

Jozy scowled, but it didn't reach his light green eyes. "Like the girls don't have you wrapped around their little fingers."

A snicker from in front of them said that their two younger brothers, Jaiseyn and Henry, had heard the exchange. Robb refrained from reminding both of them that their little sisters had no problem talking all four boys into tea parties and fashion shows. No need to bring up the past. Even if it had been just three days ago.

The meal passed without any major catastrophe. As usual, Amber ended up with food in her hair, and Alexis and Sarah fought over the last piece of pizza, but as far as eating out went, the Durands counted this one a success.

"I'm going to the restroom before we leave," Jozy announced.

"Robb, go with him," Marcile instructed her son.

"Ma, he's fourteen years-old," Robb protested.

Marcile smacked him in the back of his head. "I don't care if he's fourteen or forty, you look after your little brother."

"Yes, Ma." Robb's tone was contrite.

"Now, Jozy," Marcile turned to her second oldest son. "What do you do if someone tries anything?"

"Hex him in the crackerjacks." Jozy answered promptly. It had been one of the Durand family's first rules of self-defense for years and one that they never forgot. Robb may have been big for his age with the potential to keep growing, but Jozy was a good two to three inches shorter than average.

"Very good. I'll have Jaiseyn and Henry help me take the girls out. You two come out when you're done."

"Grown boy can't even go to the bathroom by himself," Robb muttered as he walked after Jozy. While his brother went into the restroom, Robb stationed himself outside the door and tried to look interested in the pictures hanging on the walls.

"Look what I found." A loud voice boomed next to Robb's ear, carried on a wave of alcohol too strong to have been served at this particular establishment. "I found a tiny friend."

A familiar-sounding noise – something akin to a nervous squeak – made Robb turn around. A wide-eyed and uncomfortable-looking Jozy was dwarfed under the arm of a large and inebriated man.

"Robb, help." Jozy's voice was small.

At first, all Robb could do was stare, and try not to laugh. He was already going to be in so much trouble when his mom found out about this. She'd slap him upside the head for sure if she found out that he'd laughed.

"Do you have a little friend like me?" The guy blinked blearily at Robb.

"No, but I do have a little brother who looks an awful lot like your friend." Robb withdrew his wand, hoping he didn't have to use it. With a guy this drunk, there was no guarantee that any spells Robb knew would affect him much. "Why don't you let him go?"

"But he's my friend." The man's face fell. "Who's gonna keep me company?"

"Tell you what," Robb thought fast. "Let Jozy come with me, and I'll find another friend for you."

"Okay." The man took his arm from around Jozy's shoulders. "But I want another little one with funny hair. Maybe with a leprechaun. Or a goat. One of those ones that faint."

As the boys hurried away, Robb asked Jozy, "if you couldn't hex him, why didn't you just kick him or something?"

Jozy gave Robb a fearful look. "He was huge! I don't think

one kick would've made a difference."

Robb nodded. That made sense. He paused by the host's desk and quickly explained that there was a gentleman who needed escorted out. By the time the boys reached the van, their mother wasn't in any mood to hear reasons or excuses. She simply told them to get into the van and they headed for home. It wasn't until they were almost there that Robb got the idea. He would ask their father about maybe letting him and his brothers take self-defense classes, at least him and Jozy. He knew he could explain to his father everything that had happened and not risk a smack to the head. The worst Arthur Durand would do would be to sigh. And, there was always the possibility of getting those self-defense lessons.

***

"You're going to teach us self-defense?" Robb tried to hide the disbelief in his voice.

A set of steely, pale eyes told him that he hadn't succeeded. "I've been asking your father to let me teach you boys for several months now."

Robb wasn't sure that actually answered his question, but he wasn't about to push the issue. For years, Aunt Morcades had just been a name, a vague image in pictures. It wasn't until recently that the kids had even met her. Robb was kind of glad he hadn't known her as a child. She was a bit frightening.

"We're going to start right away. I hope the four of you are in good shape." The sharp look on her face suggested that it wouldn't be good for them if they weren't.

Robb swallowed hard. He had a feeling that Aunt Morcades was going to go well above and beyond what he'd been expecting for self-defense. It would take four years before he'd find out exactly how far Morcades Durand expected him and his brothers to go, and, by then, he would be grateful for her expertise. What they would face would be like nothing he'd ever imagined possible.

Star Riders: The Twelve Introduction

My most recent novel, *Star Riders: The Twelve*, is the first in what I hope to be a series. Introducing the new characters, Tempest Black and Bram Grimm, it's a paranormal / supernatural story that explains why some characters pop up in books where they seemingly don't belong. How characters from *Reeves' Island* can show up in *The Dragon Three*. I've included the prologue and first chapter of the novel, which is from Tempest's perspective.

Prologue

The world ended in a blaze of holy light, cleansing the universe in preparation for what was to come next. Yet, even as the celebrations began, a soft command was given, and with a rustle of feathers, the appointed one took flight. The war may have ended here, but that only meant the danger for the other worlds grew. His job was clear. The twelfth must be found, the circle completed. Eleven had been left behind to stand between the darkness and humanity. If they fell, evil would consume every other world and billions of souls would be lost forever.

He closed his eyes and felt for the crack between universes. He was one of only a handful of his kind who could do this, who could travel like one of *them*.

There. He could feel it.

He stretched his arms over his head, speeding up. He tucked his wings tight against his body and began to spin. As he cut through the fabric of space, he could feel the darkness behind him. Following. Time was growing short.

He put on a burst of speed. This was not the time to worry about conserving energy. He had to reach them before they tried to go home. He had to make them see.

This was his greatest mission, the one he had been created to carry out. He could not fail.

Chapter One

Tempest

I held the flashlight between my teeth as I inserted the thin metal file into the lock. Slow inhales through my nose, slow exhales around the cheap plastic. My hands were steady, fingers never faltering as they maneuvered the workings of the lock. My pulse remained slow and regular. For all my body knew, I was relaxing with a good book, not attempting to break into my court-appointed therapist's office to read my file.

I needed to know what Dr. Rosabelle was going to recommend tomorrow so I could prepare. And by prepare, I meant figure out which way I was going to run.

I heard the security guard coming down the hallway and pushed back the sliver of panic wanting to break through. The lock clicked, and I slipped inside just as Harold, the night guard, rounded the corner. If I did my job right, no one would know I'd been here, and Harold would still have a job come morning. He was a nice enough guy; I didn't want him to get fired because of me.

I turned off the flashlight and waited for Harold to disappear down the hallway. Once I was sure he was far enough away, I turned my light back on and headed for the good doctor's computer. Her password was disturbingly easy to crack – a psychiatrist using Skinner as a password deserved to have her computer hacked. Freud and Jung got me into the patients' general folder and my personal file respectively.

Tempest Anne Black.

I skipped over the session notes. I knew what I'd told her and anything particularly important would be included in my assessment. I opened the file and began to read.

Seventeen. Mother Susanna Black, deceased. Father, unknown.

I skimmed over the medical reports of the abuse and injuries I'd sustained in my various foster homes as well as the list of arrests starting at age eight.

Been there, done that.

I didn't need a report to remind me I'd been in juvie seven times in nine years. Petty stuff. Mostly running from whatever home the state put me in, but there'd also been some B&E and one incident of hacking before I'd gotten too good to be caught.

My latest stint had been three months and I'd been out for six weeks, but was on probation, hence the weekly meetings with Dr. Rosabelle. Tomorrow, she was supposed to tell a judge if she thought they should skip the foster home, and send me straight back to juvie until I turned eighteen. No way was I going back for another seven months. Not when I kept getting thrown into solitary for defending myself.

I kept reading.

Assessment.

That's what I wanted.

Miss Black is highly intelligent, but without a measured IQ as she refuses all attempts to test her. Her poor grades are most likely the result of boredom rather than lack of understanding. Her disdain for authority figures and belief that she is the smartest person in the room also contributes to her schooling issues. Prior testing has diagnosed Miss Black as having Attention Deficit Hyperactive Disorder with Obsessive Compulsive and Narcissistic tendencies. I concur with these findings. I also believe her to be suffering from some sort of social anxiety disorder or perhaps even a form of autism. The former are all treatable with the proper medications. Therein lies the problem, as Miss Black refuses to take her medication...

I closed the file. I didn't need to read any more. I already knew what it was going to say. I needed supervision to ensure I took my meds. Meds I didn't want and was pretty sure I didn't need. Since I couldn't be trusted to take the prescribed medication, or not to run from any home I was put in, I'd be back in juvie until I turned eighteen in April.

I only half paid attention to what I was doing as I tucked my file under my arm. It'd end up in a fire at some point tonight. The other half of my brain was going over my plan. I'd always been a good multi-tasker.

I wasn't really surprised by the good doctor's findings. I knew how people saw me. Wild dark brown curls that looked like they needed tamed as much as the rest of me. Jade-colored eyes that I'd been told were arrogant and cold, which was fine with me because that wasn't a bad image to portray in my life. I was only average height, but I was strong.

Once I was safely outside, I pulled off the knit cap I'd used to prevent leaving behind any hair, and my curls tumbled out. They brushed against my bare skin, falling to bit past my shoulder-blades.

A cool breeze blew, making me wish for a moment I'd brought a coat to wear over my tank top. Autumn had come to Ohio and, with it, much cooler weather. Not for the first time, I wished my mom would've died someplace warm. At least then I would've been stuck with sunshine instead of the unpredictability of Northeastern Ohio weather. Not that I hadn't tried going someplace warmer. I'd just kept getting caught. This time, however, I was going to do what I hadn't had the courage to do before.

I was going to erase myself.

I wasn't a coward, but taking myself off the grid was extreme. When I was done, Tempest Black would cease to exist, and she was the only thing I had left of my mother, of my past. I didn't even know what my mom had looked like because the only picture of her had been taken at the morgue for their records, and I'd only seen it once. That wasn't the image I wanted in my head when I thought of her.

My lips flattened and I knew if I could see them, they'd be white. I couldn't really say I loved my mother because I'd never met her, but I'd spent enough time as a little kid fantasizing about who she'd been to love the idea of her. I never wanted to think about any of that anymore. Mourning over what might have been was stupid, and it hurt too much.

And I avoided pain at all costs.

I glanced at the Coptic cross tattoo on the inside of my right wrist. Emotional pain anyway. The physical kind actually made me feel alive. Not so much so that I'd gotten into self-harm, but I didn't exactly react to pain the way most people did. My other tattoo was partially visible under the scoop neck of my black tank. I'd gotten my favorite quote inked across my collarbone the last time I'd run. "To thine own self be true" had always resonated with me. I had plans for a couple more once I had the money.

I jogged up the stairs of the condemned apartment building where I'd been hiding since my session with Dr. Rosabelle had ended yesterday.

I pushed the other thoughts aside. I didn't have the time to be introspective. I had work to do.

No one else lived on the third floor. It wasn't exactly safe. The whole building wasn't in the best of shape, but there were parts of the ceiling on the third floor that were completely gone. I didn't really mind. It was still better than some of the other places I'd lived.

I didn't have much to pack. Another perk of being me. The one change of clothes I'd managed to smuggle out of the group home where I'd been staying, and a box that had belonged to my mom, but I could never figure out how to open. The box wasn't here though. I'd put it in a plastic bag and buried it behind the building. I couldn't take it with me now, but I promised myself I'd be back for it someday.

I left the flat pillow and threadbare blanket for the next runaway who needed a place to crash. I didn't want to take up extra room in my bag since I didn't know how far I was going, and it wasn't too cold yet. I felt a vague tug inside me, a pull I'd been ignoring for the past three weeks. I couldn't explain it, and I didn't know why it was happening. All I knew was something wanted me to go West.

When I left, I didn't look back or even bother to go by any of the dozen places I'd lived in Wycliffe. There wasn't any reason to. None of those places were home. No place was. And once I spent some time in a local internet café, I'd check out that western tug and see if I could find myself a place to disappear.

Not a home. People like me had stops, places to crash, but never homes.

Reeves' Island Short Stories

After having written *Reeves' Island*, I had people asking what happened to the kids afterwards, so I began to write short stories. I included them in the most recent edition of the novel, but earlier editions and the collection of three novels in one don't contain these stories. If you haven't read *Reeves' Island*, you might want to skip these stories.

"One Year Later"

Arisa took a deep breath as she prepared to board the plane. Her hand shook as she tucked a stray hair behind her ear.

"Nervous?" A welcomed voice spoke into her ear and she felt some of her anxiety abate.

"Aren't you?" Arisa turned to greet her boyfriend.

Will shook his head but his eyes were serious. He reached out and lightly traced the scar on Arisa's cheek – a reminder of what had happened the last time they had been on an airplane together. Arisa really didn't mind the scar. To her, it symbolized how blessed she'd been to survive the ordeal; or, at least that's what she thought most of the time. Other times, like now, it just served to remind her of how precarious life could be.

"We both agree that God wants us to go on this trip. We're going to be okay." Will took Arisa's hand in his. She nodded, still full of uncertainty. "Besides, remember what Angel said last week? That it's better to risk death knowing you're in God's plan than to lead a safe life outside His will?"

Arisa nodded. "I believe it, but I think the butterflies in my stomach are having issues."

"Come on you two. The plane's not going to wait forever." Nineteen year-old Madison McGregor walked by, carry-on tote slung over her shoulder. Her brother Trent was two steps behind. The two looked eerily alike. If Madison cut her waist length dark hair, she and Trent could almost pass for twins despite the two-year difference in their ages.

"If it makes you feel any better, I saw the pilot and he looks sane." Will grinned.

Arisa couldn't help but return the gesture. She picked up her bag and then reached for Will's hand. He squeezed her fingers and she felt her stomach cease its flip-flops. Though she was far from enjoying the prospect of flying, she breathed a prayer of thanks as she realized that she was no longer terrified. Hand in hand, Arisa and Will followed the McGregor siblings down the corridor and onto the plane.

Arisa settled into her seat, body tense as she knew it would be through the entire flight. She held onto Will's arm, resting her cheek against his shoulder. Her fingers absently ran over the jagged scar that trailed almost the entire length of his forearm, his own souvenir from their island adventure. It had been a bad wound. The Burnetts had said that only a miracle had kept infection at bay.

"We're going to be fine." Will whispered the reassurance again. He pressed his lips to Arisa's hair and prayed aloud. "Dear Lord, keep us safe and show us the work you want us to do. We know you have a purpose for us going to Sarajevo and we just ask that you show us what it is."

***

The group made its way through the once war-ravaged streets. Besides Zane McGregor and his two siblings, Living Water FMC had brought three other students: fifteen year-old Michael Thitis, thirteen year-old Deven Jordan and sixteen year-old Suria Hartz. None of the kids had really known each other well before signing up for the trip but their excitement had quickly brought them all together. Even Arisa and Will, members of another FM church, were readily accepted and became a common addition to the Living Waters youth group.

Zane stopped in front of a building that had definitely seen better days. Arisa studied the sign on the iron gate, but her limited language skills didn't allow her to understand the words. She was eager to know what they were going to be doing. Their original plan to work with one of the churches in Bosnia, but at the last minute, something had happened. They'd been rescheduled but didn't have any more information. They'd spent the first day in the foreign country doing some sightseeing and waiting for a phone call. Zane had gotten it early that morning but hadn't told the others any of the details.

"This is where we're going to be working. The orphanage

houses anywhere from fifty to seventy-five children." Zane
pushed a button next to the gate. "We're going to be cleaning,
doing some minor repairs, entertaining the children, that sort
of thing."

"Fifty kids live here?" Deven voiced what all of them were
thinking. The house just didn't look big enough.

"Good morning." A lightly accented voice drew the
attention from the building. A pleasant, but tired-looking,
woman opened the gate. "Come in." Her auburn hair was
lightly streaked with gray and she had laugh lines around
bright blue eyes.

"I'm Zane McGregor." He put out a hand. She shook his
hand as he introduced his group.

"Leann McAllister." At the curious looks, she smiled. "My
parents were missionaries from Scotland. I was born here and I
took over their work at the orphanage when they moved to
another city." She began to walk as she talked and the group
followed. "The children are just beginning their morning
classes. While they are in school, you will be working on their
play area. We would also like it if you all stayed for dinner so
you could meet the children."

The group followed Leann into the house and down a
gloomy corridor. Arisa leaned close to Will and whispered, "I
hate to think of children growing up here. I mean, I know that

it's better than other places or living on the street, but it doesn't really feel like a home, does it?"

"I know what you mean." Will agreed.

Leann took them down a set of stairs into the basement. Once the entire group was inside, she turned. "Here it is."

The room was dark, a single bulb casting a dim glow over the dreary room. The walls were bare stone, clean but unattractive. The floor was also bare, clean but ugly gray concrete. A few spindly wooden chairs sat along one wall. Several dingy stuffed animals sat in the chairs, stuffing poking out through worn spots or strained seams. A deflated basketball and deformed football rounded out the toys.

"I have a class waiting for me. My assistant will be down in a few moments. He can answer any questions you might have." Leann smiled and then disappeared back up the stairs.

"So..." Zane looked at Angel and she shrugged. "Where do you guys want to start?"

"There is paint for the walls." A new voice, deep and heavily accented, came from the stairs. All eyes turned back to the stairwell. A handsome young man entered the basement. Thick black hair, dark eyes and a warm smile. "I am Peter."

"What's with the American name?" Trent wondered aloud.

"It is not American." Peter's smile disappeared. "It is from the Bible." He looked at each member of the group as he continued. "I am Leann's assistant and I will be helping you over the next sixteen days." Arisa flushed as Peter's gaze came to rest on her. His smile returned. "And now I will ask for you to tell me your names."

***

"So, how long have you worked with Leann?" Arisa found herself between Will and Peter, painting the trim while the two men did the wider area.

"My parents abandoned me shortly after my birth. Leann found me in an alley."

"I'm sorry." Arisa felt her face get hot. She hadn't meant to bring up something painful.

"Do not worry yourself." Peter turned toward Arisa and smiled. "I am not sorry for my life, why should you be?"

"So, what exactly do you do here?" Will tried to enter the conversation.

"I do, how do you say... oh, errands. I do errands for Leann. I watch the children. Do repairs on the house." Peter returned his attention to the wall. "Anything Leann needs me to do."

"So is this what you want to do? I mean, do you see yourself here long term?" Will continued.

"I do not have much of a choice." Peter's voice was terse. "Unlike America, options are limited here."

"I didn't mean..."

"Forget it." Peter cut off Will's apology. An uneasy silence fell over the trio.

After a moment, Arisa broke it when she suddenly recalled the voicemail she'd gotten that morning. "Will, I almost forgot, I got a message from Cassidy. Sounds like some crazy stuff is going on back home."

"Everything okay?" Will's concern was evident in his voice.

"Don't know." Arisa shrugged. "The message is really short, but she didn't sound quite right."

"You are concerned for your friend." Peter drew Arisa's attention back to him. "We should pray for her. You would like that?"

"Very much." Arisa smiled.

Peter purposefully directed his statement to Arisa alone. "Then that is what we will do when we are finished here. Now, tell me of this friend of yours."

"You guys are talking a lot over there." Zane interrupted. "Hope you're getting just as much work done."

"Of course." Out of the corner of her eye, Arisa could see Peter smirking as she responded in a cheerful voice.

Peter caught her gaze and winked. "Please, continue."

***

The sounds of excited child chatter faded away as the last of the orphans were tucked into bed. Arisa sat on the bed next to a small girl with big brown eyes. Arisa smiled as she remembered back to the first night. The girl had hung back at first when the orphans met Arisa's group, but Arisa had approached and soon found herself with a shadow.

Rebecca had been at the orphanage for a few years. She'd been found, wandering the streets, barefoot and mute. Unable to tell anyone her identity, Leann had spent a year looking for the girl's family but hadn't found anything. Rebecca still hadn't spoken even though her hearing was fine and doctors could find no physical reason for her silence. She stayed at the fringes of the group, but seemed at ease in the house.

Using the bit of native language Peter had taught her, Arisa spoke. "You sleep now." Arisa smoothed the hair back from Rebecca's forehead. The little girl nodded and closed her eyes, holding tightly to the stuffed bear Arisa had given her. Arisa sat for a few minutes, waiting for Rebecca's breathing to slow. Once she was sure the girl was asleep, Arisa stood and exited the room, careful not to wake the other children.

She walked out of the back door and into the cool evening. After sixteen days of hard work, the play area was finished and the group was exhausted. They would work all day and then spend the evening with the orphans, finally dropping into their beds late at night, barely awake enough to change clothes.

Now, it was the last night and everyone was saying good-bye. The children would be in school when Arisa and her friends left. Only Leann and Peter would be accompanying the team to the airport.

Arisa stood outside, looking up at the stars. Tears pricked at her eyelids as she thought about the little girl she wouldn't see again.

"It will pain you to say good-bye." Peter came out of the shadows. "You will miss her."

Arisa didn't look away from the sky as Peter stepped up next to her. "Yes, I'm going to miss her, miss this place."

"Will you miss me?" Peter's voice was softer than usual.

Arisa looked at him, startled out of her reverie. "Well, yes... but not like that Peter." She tried to say it as gently as possible. She'd suspected his feelings but hadn't thought he'd say anything. Peter nodded, looking down at his hands. After a moment, his gaze returned to Arisa's face.

"I'm sorry." She said.

"You are in love with Will." It wasn't a question.

Arisa blushed but nodded. "I am."

"I hope he knows how blessed he is."

"He does." Will shut the door behind him.

Peter looked at Will and then at Arisa. "I will see you in the morning."

Arisa nodded but didn't take her eyes off of Will. The door clicked shut as Will closed the distance between them. They were alone.

"It's been a tough couple of weeks for you, hasn't it?" Will reached out a hand. "You've always had a soft spot for kids like this, like Rebecca. Seeing it firsthand has been difficult."

Arisa nodded and allowed Will to pull her to him. He wrapped his arms around her and she rested her head on his shoulder. "When I think about leaving Rebecca, it... my heart breaks, Will."

"I know." He pressed his lips to the top of her head. "And that's why Angel sent me to talk to you."

Arisa pulled back enough to look up at Will, the question in her eyes.

"She's been talking to Leann. Angel's going to adopt Rebecca."

Arisa felt her heart leap into her throat. "You're serious?"

Will grinned and tucked a strand of hair behind her ear. "I love watching your eyes light up like that." Arisa blushed. Will brushed his lips against hers. "And," his voice grew quiet, "I'm hoping they'll do it again." Will reached into his pocket and pulled out a box.

"Will?" Arisa stepped back.

Will took a deep breath and opened the box. He turned it to face Arisa. "I know we're young, but, these past days, watching you, seeing how much you love these kids, how much you love God. And then seeing Peter watching you and realizing that he saw those same things…" Color rose in Will's cheeks, but he continued. "It made me realize that I never want to worry that I might lose you."

Arisa put her hand over her open mouth. "Oh Will."

"Arisa," Will's voice shook. "Will you marry me?"

Arisa stared at him, eyes moving from the box with the ring to his face. His face fell and she suddenly realized that she'd been quiet too long. She shook herself out of her state of shock. "Yes."

Will's face lit up. "Yes?"

Arisa threw her arms around his neck and whispered into his ear. "Yes, a thousand times, yes."

Will pulled back enough to slide the ring onto Arisa's waiting finger. He cupped her cheek and kissed her, ring box falling to the ground, forgotten. After a few minutes, they parted. Will linked his hand through Arisa's as they turned to go back into the house.

"Just one question," Arisa stopped before they went inside. Will raised an eyebrow. "Who gets to tell my dad?"

Will chuckled and opened the door. "Your dad likes me."

"Yeah, I know." Arisa squeezed Will's hand. "You're lucky."

Will's expression grew serious. "I know."

Arisa kissed his cheek. "Come on, everyone's going to be wondering where we are." She started down the hall. He smiled as he followed her.

"Three Years Later"

The day began as clear and warm as any October day in northeastern Ohio. A bright blue sky had just the lightest feathering of clouds. Trees were beginning to turn and the scent of autumn hung in the air.

The pounding on the door woke Arisa from her light sleep. Before her brain had fully registered its wakefulness, the door opened and eighteen year-old Twila bounded inside. Arisa smiled as she remembered the reason for the excitement, the reason she was waking up in her bedroom rather than the half-empty campus apartment she and Will would be sharing.

"Come on, Arisa!" Twila jumped on the bed.

"You're awfully excited this morning." Arisa tried to sound grumpy, but the grin remained in place. She swung her legs over the side of the bed and stood.

"Hey, I just want the room." Twila bounced off the bed and darted from the room before Arisa could throw the pillow she'd picked up.

Arisa glanced at the clock on her headboard and stretched. She grabbed a towel and headed for the bathroom. When she returned to her room some time later, Twila was waiting. Her own hair and make-up was already flawless, out of place with her tear-away pants and sweatshirt. Arisa removed the towel on her head and tossed it into her hamper. She shook out her hair and sat on the floor, back to Twila.

"Are we going with two braids?" Twila took a comb and began to pick her way through her older sister's hair.

At Arisa's word of agreement, Twila separated the hair and started to work.

***

Will paced outside the door to his brother's room. Sixteen year-old Ryan was every inch the teenager when it came to valuing his sleep. Will looked at his watch again and decided that if Ryan hadn't gotten up in two minutes, he would employ more drastic measures. A cup of cold water on the feet – which usually stuck out from under the covers while Ryan's head stayed under – would do the trick.

***

"Stop fidgeting." Ryan whispered to the junior attendant. Eleven year-old Oliver McDonald opened his mouth to retort, but before he could, a sharp snap of the fingers came from the other side of the aisle. Mrs. McDonald shook her head ever so slightly and Oliver closed his mouth again.

No one noticed the exchange because the music had changed and two children were making their way down the aisle. The bride's youngest sister, fourteen year-old Josie, followed nine year-old Rebecca Michaels and eight year-old Ty McDonald. Her cheeks were pink as all eyes turned towards, her but she kept her head up and her steps slow. Behind Josie was Will's sister. Seventeen year-old Candece smiled at one of the ushers before beginning her walk. Eighteen year-old Nash White had flown in from New York City for the event. He and Will knew, though Candece did not, that her upcoming graduation gift would be a ring. The Johnsons would be having another wedding in a couple years.

A sharp intake of breath from one of the groomsmen drew chuckles from the first row of guests. Twenty-one year-old Pacey Townson's face shone as his fiancée, Cassidy Chapman, followed Candece. The sapphire blue gown looked stunning on the petite young woman. Her dark eyes sought out Pacey's blue-gray ones and friends knew they were thinking ahead to December seventh – their own wedding. Behind Cassidy was a stunning young woman in a silver dress, the material shimmering under the sanctuary lights. Twenty-three year-old Eliana Sanford-Hayes smiled at her husband as she passed. They'd been married a little over a year and, the previous night, Eliana told Arisa that they would be welcoming their first child in a little over five months. After a hug of congratulations, Arisa had laughingly thanked her matron of honor for still being able to fit into her dress.

Another groomsman – Twila's eighteen year-old boyfriend, Randy – watched the young maid of honor walk down the aisle. She caught Randy's admiring stare and blushed. As she reached the front, she turned to face the back of the church and the music changed once more. The familiar march began and the guests stood.

There, at the back of the sanctuary, holding her father's arm, was Arisa. Her dress was plain enough with little decoration. A simple beaded flower design on the bottom right of the flowing skirt was all of the beadwork and lace on the gown. The cut was fashionable and flattering, but modest. Her train was long and the veil hung past the middle of her back. The fine lace covering her face, however, could not disguise her smile or her shining eyes. She and one of the ushers exchanged a smile. Twenty-one year-old Tony stood at the back of the sanctuary, hands linked with his fiancée, Reese. All three of them knew that they and Will were remembering how this had all started. With a final nod towards Tony and Reese, Arisa signaled her father that she was ready to go. She locked eyes with Will and began her walk down the aisle.

After the words of greeting, the pastor turned to Mr. McDonald and spoke. "Who gives this woman to be married to this man?"

Mr. McDonald's voice was strong though his eyes shone with tears. "Given from God to her mother and I," he took his daughter's hands and placed them into Will's waiting ones. He looked directly at the young man and said, "and we now give her to you." Will gave a slight nod and Mr. McDonald joined his wife in the seats.

When the time came for the exchange of vows, mood set by a favorite song sung by Nat, a hush fell over the crowd. Even the restless children in the audience felt the weight of the moment and paused to listen.

Arisa took a deep breath and prayed that her voice would stay steady. "My whole life, I believed that if God wanted me to be married, He would bring the right guy to me. I had a lot of people tell me that I was too picky, that I should date anyone who was a Christian, but I knew that I wanted only God's best. And then I met you. I am always amazed at how God can take something so awful and make it so good and we're a wonderful example of that. You gave me strength when I needed it. You gave me confidence to do what needed to be done. You continue to challenge me to grow in every way. You are an awesome man of God and a continuous blessing to my life." Her voice wobbled and she brushed a hand across her cheeks. "I am a better person with you than I ever was without you. I love you, Will Johnson."

The pastor turned towards Will and nodded. Will's eyes were already shining with tears as he began. "Four years ago, God brought my family from Colorado to Ohio. And then he brought me to you. And, for me, it wasn't love at first sight because I didn't need to see you to know I loved you. I've loved you my whole life. God whispered your name into my heart even as I took my first breath. We have been promised to each other since before time began. You are God's gift to me and I will love you until the day I die."

After a moment's pause, the pastor continued. "The rings, please."

Electricity hummed through every cell of Arisa's body as she and Will repeated the age-old traditional pair of words that would join them forever. Everything around her dimmed as Will released her hands and put back her veil. He placed one hand on her waist and other on her cheek, thumb brushing her scar. Just before his lips touched hers, she heard him whisper, "forever." Her mouth curved into a smile against his kiss. After almost a full minute, the sound of applause startled her and she remembered that they weren't alone. They broke apart and turned to face the sea of faces beaming up at them.

"Friends and family," the pastor winked at Arisa as she blushed, "it is my pleasure to introduce, for the first time, Mr. and Mrs. William and Arisa McDonald."

***

Most of the guests had gone, leaving family and close friends to see off the newlyweds. Will and Arisa would be going to Toronto on their honeymoon, but they were only covering a few hours that night. They had reservations less than an hour away and would drive the remainder of the distance tomorrow. Arisa had changed out of her wedding dress and Twila had taken it, promising to put it in Arisa's bedroom until the couple returned.

"You take care." Arisa signed to her friend. Eliana and Noah would be flying back to California early the next morning. Eliana nodded and gave Arisa another hug.

"You two need to get going if you don't want to get in too late." Tony hugged Arisa and then Will. "Drive safely."

"We will." Arisa promised as she embraced Reese.

"Call when you get there." Mrs. McDonald held her daughter close. "I know you're a married woman now, but I'll still worry."

"I'll call." Arisa smiled.

"Take care of my little girl." Mr. McDonald sounded gruff, but those around knew that it was only because he was choked up.

"Always." Will's single word brought a nod from his

father-in-law.

Mrs. Johnson moved from her daughter-in-law to her son. Her eyes were red but finally dry as she reminded him to drive carefully. Mr. Johnson said nothing as he hugged Will and then Arisa. He finally had to pull his wife away, keeping one arm around her shoulders as she smiled through now tear-filled eyes.

"Thank you guys, for everything." Arisa linked hands with Will and smiled at her friends and family once more. Will echoed the sentiment and then led his bride from the reception hall and into his waiting car. The first of the stars had just begun to appear in the velvet sky as the couple drove away.

"Seven Years Later"

The villagers lined up outside the tent, patiently waiting for their chance to be seen by the doctors. As they stood, they watched the children of the Americans play with the native kids. As the day grew from warm to hot, two Americans emerged from the tent with buckets of water. The two smallest children, a blond girl and a younger redheaded boy, came running.

"They are yours?" A veiled woman spoke to the American woman who offered her a drink.

The American's green eyes lit up. She answered in heavily accented, but understandable, Arabic. "Tia is three years old and Kerr turned two last month."

"You speak Arabic." The woman seemed surprised.

"My husband and I learned in preparation for this trip. My name is Twila."

"Nazuri." The woman answered. "The girl over there is my daughter Dyni. She is ten."

"She is beautiful." Twila spoke sincerely.

"Your husband permits you to go about unveiled here?" Nazuri's curiosity overcame her timidity. "And with short hair?"

Twila smiled. She ran a hand through her hair, cropped

short to make the transition from Northeastern Ohio to the desert easier. "Most of your neighbors do not wear veils anymore." She pointed out.

"But you wear the fish." Nazuri pointed at Twila's necklace. "Do they not also believe a woman should be covered from eyes other than her husband's? Are they not even more strict about what a woman can do? My husband says that I am lucky to not be married to one of them for they treat women as slaves."

"My faith frees women." Twila answered gently. "If you would like to know more, we will be having a meeting tonight, after the sun sets."

Nazuri's voice trembled. "If the local leaders find out, they will kill everyone there. The government might say we have religious freedom, but they do not enforce it. Local religious leaders do as they wish, especially in our little village. You could all die."

Twila's smile faded, but she didn't falter. "We know. But it is worth the risk."

"Even for your children?"

Twila looked at her son and daughter. "When they were born, my husband and I gave them back to God. Whatever His will is for their lives... Randy and I put our trust in Him; even when it might cost the lives of our children."

The American's sincerity touched her. Nazuri nodded. "Dyni and I will come if we can."

Twila smiled again. "I must give the others water, but I will look for you tonight." She turned to go.

Nazuri reached out and touched Twila's arm. "Thank you, doctor."

"Randy and I aren't doctors."

"What then?" Nazuri was puzzled.

Twila chuckled. "We make movies."

***

After delivering vaccines and antibiotics until the sun disappeared, the doctors and nurses set up a space in the medical tent for the promised meeting. The handpicked team mostly came from churches the Smiths attended. A doctor and nurse came from their hometown of Wycliffe, Ohio. Two others were friends from the church in Hollywood where the Smiths went when business called them to California. The other two were volunteers from a Los Angeles church.

"How many said they would come?" The youngest of the doctors, a twenty-eight year-old pediatrician, stacked the last of the boxes in a corner. She smoothed down stray hairs as she walked over to the rest of the group.

"Five women and three men." Randy answered. He picked

up his sleeping son and carried him to a blanket at the side of the tent.

"That's good." The eldest doctor, a gentleman from Ohio, sat down and wiped the sweat from his forehead. "I wasn't sure we'd get anyone the first night."

"Here they come." Twila turned to her companions, her face shining.

This trip had been Randy and Twila's dream since Twila's sister, Arisa, had come home from her own mission's trip. After their first movie broke three box office records, they decided to make their dream into a reality. They had both been twenty-three, within a few months of each other, had a daughter and were expecting another child, but they refused to let anything get in their way. They'd faced greater odds before and knew that if this was God's will, they'd find what they needed. The media hype they hadn't wanted ended up bringing the first volunteer, a nurse from LA. The rest had quickly fallen into place and now, two short years later, they were in the Middle East, ready to distribute their faith alongside the medical treatment they financed.

After ten minutes, Randy decided to begin. All five women had come, bringing six children among them, including Nazuri with Dyni. Two of the three men had come and a couple with two children of their own had heard about the meeting from

Nazuri and joined her. Though fearful of her husband finding out, Nazuri seemed eager to hear what the Americans had to say.

"Good evening." Randy spoke in his shaky Arabic. "I am Randy Smith."

The fifty-something man to Randy's right used up his limited Arabic vocabulary. "Dr. Wesley Fredricks. I am blessed to be here."

"Dr. Cassidy Waters." The woman smiled to make up for her lack of words.

"Dr. James Waters." Her husband was only a few years older than her, but had already lost most of his hair. "Our children Deborah and Rocco." The ten and seven year-olds sat quietly with their parents, knowing it wasn't a time to play.

"Nurse Madison Nini." The smallest of the group, Madison was also one of the toughest, having lived in LA alone for fifteen years.

"Nurse Amberlee Chappell." The blond woman towered over the other women at almost six feet tall.

"Dr. Hakeem Caulfield." His teeth flashed brilliantly white against his dark skin. "Praise the Lord."

"My Arabic is bad, so I will now introduce my wife who is much better and she will speak." Randy motioned to Twila who now held their slumbering oldest child. "Twila – and our daughter Tia."

Twila smiled warmly at each person before beginning. "We are all here to offer you more than medicine. We have come here to tell you about One who offers freedom beyond anything anyone can imagine. He is the One who created all of us and He loves us more than anything else. He loves each person equally, regardless of race or gender."

She spoke for almost an hour, telling the people about their Creator and His Son. About the sacrifice for sins and the promise of eternal life. When she finished, she asked if anyone had questions.

One of the children raised his hand. "If something bad happened to you, would you still believe in this God?"

Twila exchanged a look with Randy and nodded. "Yes. When Randy and I were younger, we were in a terrible accident. Several people died." She pointed to the scar on Randy's leg. "He was shot, but God protected him. We believe that it was God's will that we survived when others did not."

"How can I know this God?" Nazuri asked.

"Me too." Her daughter spoke up.

Praising the Lord in their own native tongue, the group began to minister to their guests, using broken versions of each others' languages. They prayed together and soon the tent was filled with laughter as the new converts rejoiced. So loud were they that no one heard the approaching men until it was too late.

"What is this meeting?" An armed man shouted as he entered the tent.

"We are American doctors." Dr. Caulfield started to explain, stepping forward with palms in the air. An explosion cut off whatever he was going to say next. He looked down at the blood starting to stain his shirt and fell to his knees.

Deborah Waters was the first to scream. Kerr woke and joined in. Everything began to move in a blur of slow motion. Randy crossed the tent to pick up his son. Cassidy Waters grabbed her daughter. Two other men entered the tent. One of the village men stood. Bullets flew. People screamed. Then, it was silent as the three village leaders were the only ones left standing.

As they left, one man said to another, "burn it down. Let our people see what happens when they listen to the message of infidels."

A few seconds later, fire began to crackle and smoke seeped into the tent. From the bodies came a stifled cough. Then another from a different place. Bodies shifted and survivors emerged.

Twila pulled Tia from the rubble, unharmed. Nazuri's daughter Dyni stood up next to Tia. Both mothers had covered their daughters. Shrapnel had left numerous thin cuts all over Twila's body and a bullet had grazed her right arm, but she had survived. She didn't need to lift the hole-riddled veil to know that Nazuri had not.

"Come with me." Twila instructed Dyni. The girl nodded, still in shock.

"Twila!"

Relief flooded through her as she heard her husband's voice, followed by her baby's cry.

"Mama!"

Twila and Randy both turned and saw the children of the village couple kneeling next to their parents' bodies. Both Waters children stood behind them, bloodied, but otherwise unharmed.

"We need to leave now." One of the men from the village stood nearby, assisting one of the women who had been shot in the leg. A wound in his side bled, but he ignored it. They were the only adult survivors from their village.

"He's right." Cassidy and Nurse Chappell stood on either side of James. "The others are dead."

Twila placed Tia on one hip and took Dyni's hand. The villagers spoke to the newly orphaned children and the group carefully made its way out the back of the tent. The killers had already vanished, knowing the military would spot the fire and come looking. The overwhelmed and battered group climbed into the medical jeep and Randy drove them away from the blaze that had been so full of life only minutes before.

***

"We need to ask all three of you one more time. Do you want to come live in the United States with Randy and I?" Twila spoke to Dyni, Nami and Maku in Arabic. They answered affirmatively in English.

"Mr. and Mrs. Smith, I hope you realize that it is only because of your fame in America that we are allowing you to take three of our children. More dirt smeared on our good name is not what we need now." The government official spoke in clipped, precise English, reflecting the cold attitude Twila and Randy had been dealing with over the past weeks as they filed for custody of the three orphans. Dyni's father had immediately disowned the girl when she publicly confessed her new faith.

"I trust that the deaths of our friends is not the publicity you are referring to." Randy's eyes flashed though his tone was mild. "Or the lack of justice in their murders. Or the news that these children have been able to claim religious asylum because their lives are in danger here."

"We restate our official position we have religious freedom

and these children would be safe if they remained in their home villages." The man stiffened.

"Like our parents?" Eight year-old Maku had picked up enough English to follow the conversation. "No, sir, we go to America where we can be free to worship our God so one day we can meet our parents in heaven."

Silence fell, broken only when the overhead announcement proclaimed that their flight was boarding. The kids followed Randy and Twila, who carried their younger children. As they settled into their seats, Twila looked out at the neighboring desert. The sun cast its dying rays over the sand and as she closed her eyes, Twila could almost hear the cries in the desert. Not those of her murdered brothers and sisters who were now forever free, rather those of the lost souls, still searching for peace. She knew that, one day, she and her family would return.

"Fifteen Years Later"

The sun shone its warm afternoon rays down on the crowd gathered on the beach. The smaller children played at the water's edge as older siblings wandered, marveling at how their parents had survived for over a week before rescue planes had landed on this very beach. The adults in question watch in silence for the most part, their own memories almost too overwhelming to allow for speech. It had been twenty-six years since they'd first stepped foot onto the sand of this island and none of them had been back since. Now, as part of a promotion for the twenty-fifth anniversary of *Reeves' Island* – the major motion picture starring then teen sensations Rany Masterson and Talin Cain – they'd returned.

Forty-two year-old Will Johnson slid his arm around his wife's waist and pulled her close. Unconsciously, Arisa's fingers went to the faded scar Will had received all those years ago. Though her hair had darkened with age, and then began to lighten again as threads of gray and silver appeared, her eyes still blazed with the same intensity that had captured Will from the moment he'd seen her. The oldest Johnson child, Jesse, had Arisa's eyes. Their nineteen year-old daughter Leesha, recently married to the twenty year-old son of good friends Pacey and Cassidy Townson, had inherited her mother's personality, but her appearance fit her name. More than once, Will had wondered how much his daughter and sister would have looked alike had the latter lived. David and Leesha were only a few yards away, chatting with their seldom-seen relatives. Twila and Randy were by far the busiest of the survivors, splitting their time between their Hollywood careers and their mission work in the Middle East, all the while raising their seven children. Granted, most of their adopted children were all grown and had families of their own, but Arisa still admired her sister's energy.

"Jaci looks just like you."

Arisa turned and smiled up at Tony. He motioned towards the youngest of the Smith kids. Though he and Reese had stayed in Wycliffe, they hadn't had much opportunity to see Twila and Randy's family over the past few years.

"From what I hear, she also sounds like Arisa." Will grinned. "Twila's always complaining about how often Jaci quotes her 'favorite aunt in the whole world.'"

"Uncle Tony! Aunt Reese!" The seven year-old Johnson twins, Abul and Ani, barreled across the beach to throw themselves on their surrogate aunt and uncle. Not having children of their own, Reese and Tony had become like family to the seven Johnson children and were particularly close to the pair that Arisa and Will had adopted while visiting with

Twila and Randy overseas just a few years before.

"Don't let them get too dirty, Tony." Arisa knew her plea was futile, but she tried anyway. Though in his forties, Arisa still saw much of her childhood friend in Tony's sparkling eyes and mischievous grin.

As if called by the word that had always described him, Luke appeared, his own children in tow. While both Marieh and Joss looked like their mother Elle, it took Arisa just a few seconds to recognize the personality of Luke White. Not more than a foot behind Luke was, as always, Kris and his own children. The moment he released their hands, Luke's namesake and his sister Emma made a beeline for Marieh and Joss, and the foursome took off into the water.

"Elle's going to kill me." Luke sighed as the kids didn't even pause to remove their shoes.

"Where is she?" Arisa glanced around.

"Helping her friend Tex. Something about another problem with goats in Arkansas." Luke shrugged. "I didn't quite catch the whole thing." He grinned and then added, "I also probably didn't hear it right."

"Elle still doesn't like to fly, does she?" Arisa watched as her dark-haired son tried to climb onto Tony's back without any help.

Luke shook his head. "Nope. I can't get her on a plane."

"How goes the comic book business?" Tony asked, swinging Ani onto his shoulders.

"Good." Kris's hand rose to his face to push back the glasses he no longer wore. "WIT Publications just hired us to do the graphic novels for *Tru Shepard* and *The Dragon Three*."

"Adalayde and Emily will be thrilled." Arisa gestured towards two teenagers who were attempting to discreetly watch Will's nephews. Ryan's son Connor and Candece's son Nikolas were pretending not to notice the girls' attentions, but failing miserably. Arisa felt a moment of amusement at how some things never changed. "Nat tells me her girls are huge fans those books."

"Speaking of books," Luke directed his attention towards Arisa. "I hear your latest one is doing well."

"It helps when you own a bookstore."

"It also helps to be talented." Will interjected.

"Someone's a bit biased." Arisa rolled her eyes.

After a few more minutes of idle chitchat, Arisa excused herself and headed inland, stepping just inside the tree line. She leaned back against a large truck and closed her eyes. The crash of the oceans on the shore muffled the noise of people into nonsensical white noise, a rhythmic sound that didn't require any interaction on her part. Arisa opened her eyes, sensing Will before she heard him.

"Are you all right?"

He knew her so well. He always had.

Arisa shook her head. "We almost died here. Some of us did." For a moment, she saw the faces of those who had died. The teacher and her child who hadn't returned home. Those who'd been buried at sea. The one who'd made it back to Wycliffe to be laid to rest. The forever young who never had the chance to grow up, to become whatever they'd wanted to be.

Will reached for his wife, threading his fingers through hers. "But we survived. We made it." He raised their linked hands and lightly kissed the back of her hand. "Come on, let's go get the kids and go home."

Arisa leaned her head against Will's shoulder as they began walking back towards the beach. "Home sounds good." She breathed in the salty air and straightened. "Home sounds very good."

The Last Summer Short Stories

Shortly after publishing the original edition of *The Last Summer*, a friend of mine and I were talking about some of the things not included in the book, specifically, the stories from outside during the last few weeks. When I told the same friend that I was working on a new edition of *The Last Summer*, and asked what he'd like to see, he said he wanted to know about what had happened outside when the comet came.

The first bit that follows is the short story I wrote for that friend, and yes, I went a little meta, but it was just written in fun for him. I wasn't trying to pull a Stephen King or *Supernatural*. I tweaked it a bit, but it remains otherwise unchanged. In the last one, you may recognize names of characters from other books. If you've read *Star Riders: The Twelve*, you know how those characters ended up here.

Both of these stories only appear in the newest editions of the novel, but not in previous editions or in the three-in-one collection released in 2015.

"The Gift From Before"

The flickering light from the television cast an eerie glow on the otherwise darkened room. River didn't need any illumination, however, to see Jericho sitting on the couch. Over the past year, he'd grown so aware of Jericho that he could find her almost anywhere. Now, he crossed the room and sat down next to her on the couch.

"Is Ardra in your room?" River slipped his arm around Jericho's shoulders and pulled her to him. She nodded, snuggling up against him. "Emmanuel's in mine. We can work out more permanent living quarters tomorrow, you know."

"I know." Jericho's voice was muffled.

"Then what's wrong?" River pressed his lips against Jericho's hair.

Jericho pulled back and looked up into River's concern-filled eyes. "Emmanuel gave me something." She reached down beside her and picked up a rectangular package. She peeled back the wrapping to reveal two books. Before River could ask, Jericho held up a sheet of paper and began to read.

"'My dear daughter, I truly hope that this letter finds you well. I suspect that it will and that it will find you with River at your side. I will always be grateful to God for bringing the Colemans into our lives. Ardra and Emmanuel were to give this to you as soon as they saw you. We consider ourselves blessed in the lottery as two more members of the Coleman and Mann families will survive. In the package, you'll find two books. Before you read them, there's a story to how they came to be in my possession...'"

***

Leo Mann entered the bookstore without really knowing why. He was actually surprised that the store was open at all. With only a few weeks left, most businesses weren't even bothering. Both the Mann and Coleman families were preparing to move into their church and Leo was getting the last of what they needed. Having spent so much of his life reading, he supposed that's what had prompted him to go into the store for reading supplies. As he turned down one row of books, he noticed that the store wasn't as empty as he'd originally thought. A short woman in her late twenties and a thin young man, appearing to be a few years younger, stood at the end of the row, deep in conversation. Leo started to return his attention back to the books when he realized that he'd recognized one of the pair. He looked again, stepping closer and catching part of their conversation.

"So I figured what better way to pass the time than reading as much as possible." The woman smiled up at her friend.

"Did you see that they moved your book to the bestsellers

section?" The young man plucked a volume from the shelf.

As soon as Leo saw the cover of the book, he realized why he'd recognized the woman. Jericho owned several books by this particular author and had, in fact, gone to a book signing in nearby Fort Collins a few years ago. He stepped forward, drawn more by the connection to his daughter than by anything else.

"Excuse me?"

Two pairs of eyes turned towards Leo.

"Are you Victoria Perkins? The author?"

The woman nodded and smiled. "Yes. And this is my friend, Mark Klinger. He's an author as well." She held out a hand and Leo shook it. "And you are?"

"Leo Mann. My daughter, Jericho, is a huge fan."

Victoria smiled. "Thank you."

"Wait a minute." Mark turned towards Leo "Jericho Mann is your daughter?"

"Yes." Leo knew immediately what was coming next.

"*The* Jericho Mann?" Victoria's eyes widened.

Leo nodded. Mark and Victoria exchanged glances that Leo couldn't understand.

Victoria reached into her bag and pulled out two hard-backed books. Mark handed her a pen. As she spoke, she scribbled something on the inside cover of one of the volumes.

"Mark and I were in town to get the first editions of our newest books. Obviously, there's no point in publishing anything now, but the editor's a friend of mine, so the publisher made a copy of mine for me and one of Mark's for him."

"Ok." Leo was puzzled, but let the author continue.

"This is going to sound strange, but since you said your daughter enjoyed my books, if you can figure out a way to get these to her, we'd be grateful." Victoria extended her hand, now holding both books. "It'll be nice to know that something of ours will be there for future generations to enjoy."

Leo nodded and took the books, thanking the authors before hurrying away, tears pricking at the corners of his eyes.

***

"'...so I passed the books on to Ardra and Emmanuel. Read them. Enjoy them. And pass them on.'" Jericho's voice trembled as she continued, "'And now, my beloved child, I must say farewell. I will not draw this out as we have already said our good-byes. You know that your mother and I are proud of you and we have great faith that you will always remember what we've taught you. We know where your heart lies and we will see you again in heaven. Until then, stay true to God and to what He tells you to do. Love always, Dad.'"

River cupped Jericho's chin and tipped her face up to look

at him. Without a word, he bent his head and kissed away Jericho's tears. He touched his lips to hers, wanting nothing more than to kiss away the pain as he had her tears. When he pulled back, Jericho's eyes were dry. She rested her head on his shoulder as he reached for the larger of the two books, flipping it open to read the inscription.

"'We often find love and strength where we least expect it. Words can show us truth when nothing else can. Please, pass on the truth of stories to those who survive. Do not let the written word die away with the rest of the world. God bless you as you carry on. Victoria Perkins.'" River turned the book over to examine the cover. A single golden eye adorned the bright green dust jacket. In elegant script was written *Dragon Eyes* by Victoria Perkins.

Jericho opened the second book and read out loud. "'May the words you read in these pages give you courage in the dark hours to come. Mark Klinger.'" She turned the page and continue to read. "*In Our Darkest Hour* by Mark Klinger. Chapter One..."

***

"Do you have everything?" River whispered in his wife's ear.

Jericho nodded. She tucked the two well-worn volumes into

her bag and slung the bag over her shoulder. It was time to head to the doors. Time to return home.

"Final Impact"

There were only minutes left and they could all hear the crashing of falling debris and the screams from outside, muffled by the walls but still audible over the soft sounds of the people inside the church.

Will's mother was holding his thirteen year-old brother while his father had Candece. They sat across from him and he could see the calm on their faces. It didn't surprise him. He and his family had been one of the last to move into the church, and he hadn't been sure at first that it was a good idea. The atmosphere here had changed his mind. There was none of the fear that had permeated the outside. They were at peace.

"It's almost over, Sweetie. Just close your eyes."

A woman's soft voice drew his attention and he looked up. A family was huddled together next to his. No, he amended. Two families, though they looked like they'd known each other before. The little girl being soothed on her mother's lap was clutching a stuffed black and gray dog. He was suddenly and painfully reminded of Leesha at that age.

He swallowed hard, a lump forming in his throat. He missed his little sister. He took a breath. He wasn't going to cry. He wanted to go out as strong as his parents, as the rest of the people around him.

A hand slipped into his and he looked down at a newly familiar face. He'd met Killeen when she'd greeted his family when they'd first arrived. Her mother had accidentally ODed right after the announcement in August and Killeen moved in to the church a few days later. She and Will had bonded quickly and he was glad she was with him at the end.

"You know who they are?" She leaned her head on his shoulder. "They're the families of the kids who spotted the comet. You'd think they would've let them all go to the caves for that, wouldn't you?"

Will nodded, stealing another look at them. He'd thought he'd seen them before somewhere. The paparazzi had been brutal to them. Granted, the media had been bad with all of the families of the pre-selected, but the Mann and Coleman families had been hit particularly hard. Will was just grateful that when Leesha's name had been selected in the lottery, no one had hounded them. The Manns and Colemans hadn't even gotten to have that in peace. One of the last news stories yesterday had been about how they'd each had a child selected.

His eyes found the boy who'd give his place to his twin brother. The story was that the twin who hadn't been selected had been in love with the girl who'd been chosen, so that one had given up his place. Will shook his head. He couldn't imagine being in that young man's position.

The boy – Al, Will suddenly remembered – was holding a pair of girls who didn't look much younger than his own brother and sister. Will wrapped his arm around Killeen's shoulders. He could feel the tension radiating from her and understood.

They'd talked and he knew she was at peace with what was coming, but that didn't make the anticipation any easier.

There was a loud crack and the building shook. Some of the younger kids cried out. A rumbling sound filled the air and everything became suddenly sharp and clear.

A pair of sisters with the last name Juniper clung to each other.

One of the Coleman girls buried her face against her father's chest.

A young man named Kase held a petite young woman whose name Will had never gotten.

Will's eyes met his mother's even as Killeen's arms squeezed him so hard that he almost couldn't breathe. He and his parents had already said all they needed to say to each other. His mother's eyes were shining with unshed tears, but there was no fear in them and she gave Will the strength to not be afraid as the roar grew closer, reverberating in his chest, hurting his ears.

He closed his eyes and tilted his head up towards the sky as his world disappeared.

Coming Soon:

Star Riders: Nevermore

Book Two in the paranormal / fantasy series

that began with *Star Riders: The Twelve*.

Other books by Victoria Perkins

Reeves' Island

The Last Summer

Three, Two, One

My Immortal, 'm Cara

This Weak & Idle Theme

The Dragon Three

Star Riders: The Twelve

Thank you for reading and I hope you enjoy. If at all possible, please leave a review somewhere, even if it's to say what you didn't like. Thank you for your support.

You can find more information about me, as well as my books at my official website www.vpbooks.com, on Amazon, or various social media sites. I appreciate interaction from readers and always try to respond promptly. Thank you again.

Made in the USA
Lexington, KY
16 July 2017